ILLUSION OF LOVE

Joan Garrison

Indigo Norden is an opportunist – an exploiter of women, a picker of brains and talent, a man who uses his male magnetism and killer instinct to convince Abby Young to ghost write the technical papers which he hopes will land him in the executive suite. And Abby, eager to win Indigo's love and a secure marriage, did not realize that love was only an illusion, and that Chet Ballantine, the company's brilliant engineer and inventor, was offering her the real thing.

ILLUSION OF LOVE

Joan Garrison

Curley Publishing, Inc.
South Yarmouth, Ma.

Library of Congress Cataloging-in-Publication Data

Garrison, Joan, 1916–
    Illusion of love / Joan Garrison.
        p.   cm.
    1. Large type books.   I. Title.
[PS3527.E598I4   1990]
813′.54—dc20
ISBN 0–7927–0243–3 (lg. print)   89–38780
ISBN 0–7927–0239–5 (pbk.: lg. print)   CIP

Published in Large Print by arrangement with Donald MacCampbell, Inc. in the United States, Canada, the U.K. and British Commonwealth.

Distributed in Great Britain, Ireland and the Commonwealth by CHIVERS LIBRARY SERVICES LIMITED, Bath BA1 3HB, England.

Printed in Great Britain

ILLUSION OF LOVE

Chapter One

The thief was a cadaverous man with the cheeriest, most innocent blue eyes Abby Young had ever seen. Her first impulse was to scold the detective who'd brought him to her office. Duty might be duty, she thought, but why humiliate a person by parading him in handcuffs? Then, smiling sweetly, the thief told the detective, "Some day, bub, I'm gonna kick your teeth down your throat." The grating menace in his voice drew Abby's nerves taut. She changed her mind about scolding the detective. It was just possible, she decided, laughing at herself, that he knew his job better than she knew it.

The detective drew some papers from his briefcase and pushed them across the desk. "These were found in his room," he explained. "They've got the library stamp on them, but my wheel thought you should check them."

Abby skimmed through the papers, checking by means of code numbers. When there was no possible justification for doubt, she nodded. "They're ours, all right," she reported. She looked unhappily at the thief.

1

"I don't understand this at all, really I don't. These papers cover a can-opener that's been in the public domain for years. We keep them for reference purposes only. You could've bought such a can-opener for a quarter in any grocery store in town."

"Just maybe, sis, I'm being framed. Like you said, why should I want them papers?"

The detective returned the papers to his briefcase. "Would you happen to recognize this guy, Miss Young? Maybe he's been in here looking through your books."

"No."

"That's a pretty fast decision, isn't it?"

"Not at all, really. This is a technical library, you see. Only personnel of the company are admitted to the stacks. Oh, we accord courtesy privileges to other technical and scientific people in town, but they must have a card signed by Mr. Norden and countersigned by an officer of the company they work for. I know the people who work here and most of the outside people as well."

"Sis," the thief asked, "couldn't anybody, just anybody, make a stamp like yours and —"

"We use a special code number," Abby interrupted. "I identified the papers by the code number, not by the stamp. I'm sorry, sir, but if I must identify those papers in a courtroom, I can do so easily and completely."

2

The detective zippered the briefcase shut. "I'm under orders to take this guy to one of your wheels," he grumbled. "It's all screwy to me. I go out and risk my neck to catch a thief; then I'm ordered to bring him here for who knows what."

"Some of the work at Better Ways, Incorporated, is involved with the national defense effort. Did you want a particular wheel, or will just any wheel do?"

"Character named Mikel."

"Around here," Abby briefed him tactfully, "Mr. Mikel is known as the executive vice president. It's likely he'll be named president when Mr. Wente moves up to head the board of directors."

Abby pressed her call button. There was a long wait, during which the thief stirred uneasily. Presently Linda Aley came in. Linda spotted the handcuffs almost immediately, and her mouth dropped agape. Abby ordered crisply: "Take these gentlemen to Mr. Mikel's office, Linda. I think you'd better use the back stairs."

The detective tipped his cap and took the thief by the arm. The thief looked angry enough to spit. He did spit just as they left Abby's office . . .

Abby waited, a slim woman of twenty-four, her golden hair done up in a coronet, her blue

3

eyes puzzled and thoughtful under her bushy, unplucked brows. Figuring it would take less than five minutes for Indigo Norden's private grapevine to get the news of the arrest to him, she assembled the papers she was sure he'd want to see and then put the instant-coffee water on to boil. But these were almost routine, mechanical acts. Her mind gnawed busily away at the mystery even while she performed them. Why in the world, she wondered, had an obviously uneducated person broken into the library and rummaged through the files and walked off with those particular papers and schematics but nothing else? And why . . .

Her mind never got any further. Two minutes sooner than she'd expected him, big Indigo strode in and favored her with a kiss on the left cheek. "I may marry you," he announced. "I don't know why a fellow would be silly enough to marry a beautiful and intelligent woman, but I may marry you."

"It would be kind, Indigo."

He dropped onto a chair and sat with lips pursed while she made his coffee and added the correct amount of sugar and powdered cream. For some preposterous reason, Abby felt tense and worried until he'd tested the coffee and pronounced it drinkable. Abby hated the flood of relief that ran through her.

4

No woman on earth, she thought somewhat bitterly, should allow an Indigo Norden to mean so much to her. If they *didn't* marry this year, she'd quit and head for New York. There were always good jobs available for thoroughly trained technical librarians. There were always men available, too, for any willing woman under ninety-nine.

"I understand," Indigo said, "that they've caught your thief."

"Well, they brought in a man they say is the thief. But I've watched so many Perry Mason things on television I automatically sit back and wait for proof and conviction."

"Evidence?"

"Two sets of papers, Indigo. The first set covered that O'Malley can-opener they still sell in supermarkets and such. I made much of the fact the plans are in the public domain. The other set of papers was something else again, as I said in my memo to Mr. Wente. The basic paper is a schematic for an electronic television aerial. I don't know if you're familiar with the project, but the firm is sponsoring an inventor who thinks such an aerial can be built into a television set."

"Big deal?"

Abby mixed coffee for herself. "Well," she said carefully, "you're familiar with the temperament of inventors. They're born

5

optimists. I suppose they must be to tackle the problems that baffle ordinary people such as I. It could be a big deal, I suppose. For example, the idea behind the invention is to project a continuous beam to infinity. The television transmission signal is supposed to be intercepted by the beam and be pulled into the set by electromagnetic means."

"Why's that such a big deal?"

Abby knew better than to be startled by the question, but she was. Now, as always, it seemed incredible to her that a man with no understanding or appreciation of the engineering and electronic arts could head the promotion department of a firm such as Better Ways, Incorporated.

"The key word I gave you," she explained, "is infinity. Television signals aren't bounced back to earth by the ionosphere, as radio signals are. They go out in a straight line, forever and ever through space. Hence the idea of bouncing the signal from communications satellites. But if this inventor's electronic aerial works, anyone anywhere could pull in a television signal from any place on earth. See how big it is?"

Indigo grunted. "Nuts. A deal like that must've been explored and discarded years ago by RCA and Westinghouse and others. Those boys aren't dopes."

"Of course not. Still, it was an individual, not a corporation, that developed the cathode-ray tube. And people can stumble onto things. How did Firestone discover his method for the vulcanization of rubber?"

"You think the thief was after that particular set of papers, is that it?"

"No. I'm simply pointing out that many goodies were overlooked to get the can-opener and aerial papers."

He put his cup on her desk. A natural-born pacer, he began to pace to and fro between the desk and the windows overlooking Goose Point Bay. He did his best thinking, he always claimed, when he was pacing, as if the joggling of his physical system also joggled his thinking apparatus.

"We'll sit on it," he decided quickly. "I'll huddle with the legal department. I wonder if we could classify the aerial thing. That would kill off any discussion of the contents of the papers in the courtroom."

"It might be well to propose that, Indigo."

"Write a memo for my signature, will you? But you'll have to brief me on your argument afterward. It seems that not everybody up in the executive suite wants me to be a vice president. Cleary never misses a chance to make me look bad on technical or scientific matters."

7

"Actually, Indigo, this is an administrative matter. The firm's invested about ten thousand dollars in the project. If it were discussed in open court, some other firm would get the benefit of the information developed by the inventor with our money. If the papers are given a classification of 'secret,' they won't be discussed in open court and our investment will be protected. How could Mr. Cleary make you look bad on a dollar-and-cents issue?"

"Still –"

Abby astonished herself by saying quickly and vehemently, "No, sir." Having said the words, she looked at her engagement calendar. "Also, I'm behind in my work, Indigo. That detective used up a lot of time."

"Now, now, now."

But having managed just once to refuse him a favor, Abby ignored the charm of his twinkling gray eyes and broad, bright, faintly boyish smile. She flicked the intercom switch and called to her secretary, "Please send Mr. Ballantine in, will you?"

"Now just a moment," Indigo snapped. "I hate to pull rank on anyone, but I do think I have the authority to order you to write that memo."

"No, Indigo. This is the technical library,

and I'm the librarian in charge. My function is to operate a service for our engineers and scientists, not to write memos for various department heads."

"And all this just because I took Deanna Mikel to the ballet?"

Abby flushed; she couldn't help it.

"Be a big girl," Indigo ordered. "There's that vice presidency coming up, and I'd like it. Her father is our executive vice president, in case you've forgotten. He does the nominating."

"That isn't the way to get ahead!"

"Rubbish." He was up and pacing again, hands thrust into the pockets of his charcoal-gray silk trousers. "You get ahead any way you can," he rumbled. "I'm proof of that right now. Look, you have to assume all your competition is just as able as you are. So you have to work in the little extras that count. Call it apple polishing or courting the right girl at the right time or whatever else you want to call it. The fact is, I'm an individual to Mikel for the simple reason I'm an individual to Deanna."

"Write your own memo," Abby said bluntly. "I'm not an idiot, you know. You use me for the writing, you use her for the contact, and how many other women do you use around here, and for what purpose?"

"Maybe ten, maybe twenty," he said coolly. "And I use them for the only purpose that counts – getting myself up to an office in the executive suite."

"Aren't you proud of yourself?"

"Not yet, frankly. Eighteen thousand a year is pretty good for most fellows, but it isn't good enough for me. I take it you want to be crossed off my list?"

Abby drew a deep breath.

The pacing ended. Big Indigo Norden turned and looked her dead in the eye. "You do that memo, or I'll cross you off the list, Abby. I kid you not."

"I won't be used that way!"

Indigo headed for the door. "You heard me," he said. "That's that."

The door opened as he neared it, and Chet Ballantine came in with such boyish eagerness that Indigo had to grin. "You may win her yet," he told Chet. "Keep pitching, Ballantine. Strange things happen in this world, believe me."

Then Indigo went out booming laughter, while Abby had to fight to keep herself from picking up a book or something and throwing it at him.

Chapter Two

Chet Ballantine thought that the sea air might do her some good, so he walked Abby home that evening by way of the shore road. As they reached Water Street, a great freighter nosed in from the Atlantic Ocean and pushed slowly but powerfully by them en route to the docks beyond Goose Point Bridge. The freighter looked considerably the worse for wear. Great rust splotches could be seen the length of its starboard keel, while its superstructure looked as if it hadn't been painted in years. Chet, a quality-minded man who resented anything shoddy or shabby, wagged his head disapprovingly. "This country had better start shaping up," he said. "Our merchant marine's a disgrace. What will happen if another war comes along and we're short of cargo ships?"

"We'll build new ones, I suppose."

"Certainly. As we did in World War I and World War II. Crash program. Spend ten times as much money to build short-lived junk as we'd have to spend right now to build a quality fleet. The thinking's wrong, Abby. When a tiny nation like Greece is allowed to become the major merchant-marine power of the world, our thinking is dangerously wrong."

"What would you do if you had the power?"

"Subsidize our merchant marine heavily for the same reason we now subsidize agriculture. Food and ships are essential to national security."

Abby buttoned her coat against the cool October sea air. She supposed, studying the sky, that it wouldn't be many weeks before the first snow came flying down to transform Cantwell, Massachusetts into the traditional winter wonderland of deep drifts and sparkling icicles. For some reason, the prospect troubled her. Then the reason the prospect troubled her popped into her mind, and that troubled her, too. Last year at this time, she recalled, she'd honestly believed she was beginning her final year as head technical librarian at Better Ways, Incorporated. She'd been so positive she'd be married by now that last October she'd begun to train Alice Hull to succeed her.

Her change of mood was noticed and deplored. "I think you dream too much, hope for too much," Chet said gruffly. "Facts are better than dreams."

For a moment, Abby disliked him. She

retorted sharply, "Coming from an inventor, of all people, that sounds odd!"

"It shouldn't sound odd, not to a technical librarian who has some notion of how inventors work. We don't dream. We simply notice a need for a device or for an improvement of a device already on the market. Based on careful, even scientific investigation, we decide exactly what's needed and how to go about developing the thing that's needed. Then it's work, hard work, until the thing is finally developed. No dreams, you see; none at all."

They came to a bench, and Chet gave every indication of wanting to sit down and smoke his pipe and hold hands. But with the Norden ultimatum to consider, Abby was anxious to get to her room in Washburn House and do some brilliant thinking before the dinner bell rang. If she decided that surrender were necessary or advisable, then she'd have to get to work on that pesky memo. Even with the best of luck, she'd not finish the memo before midnight. Whenever you wrote a memo that Mr. Cleary was sure to examine for any possible weakness, you had to write as tightly as any lawyer composing a brief.

"Why don't I go on alone?" she proposed. "I can't be good company, Chet, and I really don't have much time."

"Norden's cracked the whip, and you must hop?"

Abby whirled on him. Too furious to speak, she glared.

At twenty-eight, however, Chet Ballantine wasn't a man to be routed or even discomfited by a woman's glare. A graduate of M.I.T., possessed of his Master's, a sound and industrious mechanical engineer earning fourteen thousand a year, he was comfortably at home in the world and sublimely confident of his ability to cope with any and all problems the world posed for him.

"I had to say that," he told her unapologetically. "Norden's a familiar type to anyone who's been in this profession longer than a year. He has drive; he's a born opportunist; he's a born picker of brains and talent. What he doesn't know about technical or scientific theory and fact would fill a thousand libraries, but he's clever enough to exploit women like you, using that male magnetism he was blessed with. All right. More power to him as long as he doesn't hurt you."

"Chet, will you please, please, *please* let me decide what's good for me and what isn't?"

Crossly, before he could say another word, she swung about and hurried alone on Water Street to Goose Point Bridge. Crossing the

14

bridge, with the wind buffeting her and the water foaming and crashing far below, she gave thought to the idea of crossing Mr. Chet Ballantine off *her* list. Her good angel deliver her, she thought fervently, from men who professed to know exactly what a woman should or shouldn't do with her life!

She reached big, brown-shingled, gable-windowed Washburn House at twenty minutes to six. Mail was waiting for her on the cherry drum table in the old-fashioned tiled vestibule, and after she'd gone into the living room to read her letters before the fire, Mrs. Kurzen came in with the traditional cup of chicken broth and crackers spread with cream cheese and chopped black olives. "Nice day?" Mrs. Kurzen asked, as usual. "Around here it was pretty dull. Sometimes I think I should've finished high school. It must be pretty nice to work in a library or an office."

"The grass is always greener on the other side of the fence," Abby reminded her bitterly. She tried the broth. It was quite good and piping hot. Two or three sips, and the fire crackling cheerily across the room, filled her with a sense of well being. Relaxing, she studied the small, gray-haired, brown-eyed, strong-chinned Mrs. Kurzen. "I don't think it's ever too late to broaden one's education," she told the woman. "But what you do with an education after you've acquired it – well, that's another matter. I could use a good technical typist, for instance. I'd not pay as well, though, as the salary you're earning here."

Heavy, regularly spaced, piston-like thumps sounded on the carpeted stairs. Colonel Delaney all but marched in for his own broth before the fire. He nodded shortly. "Good day at the office?" he asked. "I never was a desk man myself, but I understand some people don't mind."

"Colonel," Mrs. Kurzen asked, "if you was me, would you go back to high school?"

"What in the world for?"

"So maybe I could be something better than a mule in a boarding house."

"Rubbish."

Colonel Delaney settled down in the wing chair to the left of the fireplace. He adjusted the black patch over his right eye, then filled his pipe. "I find," he told Mrs. Kurzen, "that all this fuss about making money is for people Miss Young's age. The older I grow, the less sure I become that material things matter. But that's an old man's view of things, I suppose."

Mrs. Kurzen gave him his broth. "Just have one cup," she advised them. "Tonight I'm serving corned beef and cabbage. It's funny,

16

but I could always do corned beef and cabbage pretty good."

Mrs. Kurzen checked the room, returned two or three magazines to the table and hustled out.

"Sally Washburn's been talking to her," Colonel Delaney explained. "I think that at high school, the seniors are being exhorted to go on to college. Sally comes home and passes on the pep talks to Mrs. Kurzen."

Abby smiled politely and turned back to her mail.

Colonel Delaney ignored the hint. "I'm glad I found you here alone, Miss Young," he said doughtily. "I've been wanting to have a serious chat with you about Sally Washburn."

"Colonel, I –"

"If she were a boy, there'd be no problem, none whatsoever. I'd pop her into the U.S. Military Academy at West Point. Good stuff in her, and they'd bring it out. But women – well, they're not men."

"Colonel, I've had a busy day, and I have a major decision to make before I go to bed. If you don't mind, I'd rather not become involved in Sally's problems."

He wasn't offended, as she'd feared he would be. Nor was he silenced, either.

"That's the typical selfishness of today talking," he said bluntly. "These days,

17

people seem to have time only for their own problems. I wonder why that is. All the opportunities open to you people of today were earned for you by a generation that cared enough about others to work for the benefit of others."

Sighing, Abby put her mail into her handbag. "I suspect," she said waspishly, "that's how you won your famous military victories in World War II. You didn't outsmart the enemy; you just wore him down."

He grunted.

"What's Sally's problem, Colonel?"

"Hasn't found herself, that's the problem. All froth, no substance. I talk to her mother, but you know her mother. And that half-sister of hers! I can't understand June these days. Before she married that big-time lawyer, she was a social worker who had time for everyone's problems, Sally's included. But now –"

"How old is Sally?"

"Seventeen."

"The Washburns must do well here."

"Doubtless. Fifteen boarders, most of them too elderly to eat much. But what has that to do with Sally?"

"Simple. If you don't have to fret about money, the chances are you'll mature rather late. For instance, I did have to fret about money. I knew I couldn't go to college without scholarships, so I applied myself from my freshman year on."

"I was thinking, Miss Young, that if Sally could work part-time under a woman like you –"

"No. Colonel, you won't approve, I realize, but I'm not interested in establishing a personal relationship with Sally Washburn. Candidly, this is just a place I live in for so many dollars every month. It isn't my home, as it appears to be your home."

He lit his pipe. The tobacco had a nice aroma that went well with the smell of burning oak. "I do wish you'd think about it," he said insistently. "There must be something a bright girl could do there."

"If there were, Colonel, I'd telephone someone in welfare work and ask her to send me a girl who urgently needed a helping hand."

That did stop him.

While he was thinking it over, the telephone rang in the hall. Mrs. Kurzen answered, then poked her head into the great living room. "For you, Miss Young. It's that Mr. Norden."

"Not in."

"But I told him –"

"Still, Mrs. Kurzen, I'm not in."

Mrs. Kurzen wagged her head and pulled the door shut again.

"Good for you," Colonel Delaney said briskly. "I know men, if not women. I've not been happy about your apparent infatuation with Mr. Norden."

"*You've* not been what?"

He wagged a forefinger at her. "Now you stop being a loner, young lady," he ordered. "You should've done a duty in the Army. You'd have learned the futility of trying to be a loner. Whether you like it or not, others exist and will take an interest in your affairs – have views on them, among other things. Why are you living here if you don't care about others and don't want others to notice you? All the other boarders are retired folks like myself. We haven't much to do, so we mind one another's business."

"So I'm beginning to see."

"I'm not sure I approve of your inventor, either," Colonel Delaney declared. "Seems to be a decent enough young man, but what are his prospects? Everyone knows inventors seldom get anywhere."

Abby fled to her room, sure that if she didn't she'd be rude. Yet there was a comical aspect to the old man's interest in her affairs: he was just as unhappy about her involvement

with Indigo Norden as she was at the moment!
So?

Abby sat on the quilted bedcover and looked steadily out the window at the sky. She did the thinking she'd wanted to do, and when the sensible decision occurred to her mind, she accepted it without quibbling. She went directly to the telephone and called Indigo to give him the news she'd written too many memos for him to write this memo now.

Frighteningly, Indigo Norden just grunted and broke the connection.

Chapter Three

Abby neither saw nor heard from Indigo until Friday afternoon. That surprised her, because late Tuesday morning her assistant, Alice Hull, came in from the library with an interesting tale of upper-echelon warfare between a faction headed by Indigo and a faction headed by Mr. Patrick Cleary. Alice brought a pot of tea and two cups and sat down as if for a long gossip session. "That thief," she began her tale, "has precipitated quite a hassle. Mr. Wente is all for prosecution and a long prison term. Mr. Cleary backs him.

But Mr. Norden says the publicity might be harmful. And guess what?"

"What?"

"When Mr. Cleary challenged him to demonstrate how prosecution would be harmful, Mr. Norden asked him outright if he'd ever held a public relations job."

"Clever. When you can't defend, attack."

"Well, our executive vice president surprised Mr. Wente and Mr. Cleary by saying he could see no point in paying a promotion specialist eighteen thousand a year for advice no one appeared to want. Along about then, according to Mr. Wente's secretary, Mr. Cleary just about had pups. Mr. Cleary said it seemed reasonable to him to ask even a specialist to justify his conclusions. Mr. Cleary said that even engineers and scientists are expected to justify all the conclusions they make in their technical and scientific reports."

Abby tried the tea. She liked it. "How come you're not married, either?" she asked Alice. "If I could even boil water properly, I'd be married by now."

"All the men I know like coffee, I guess. The upshot of the conference was that not later than tomorrow afternoon Mr. Norden would present a paper justifying his argument that prosecution of the thief would be harmful

22

to the best interests of the corporation."

Abby whistled softly. The development took her by surprise, and she didn't care who knew it. "How's Indigo going to do that?" she asked. "He has about as much knowledge of the technical matters involved as I have of baseball."

Alice asked, in turn, quite casually, "Have you ever heard of Rose Lovadero?"

"Who?"

"She's a technical writer assigned to the kitchen appliance department. She's very good, I understand. I understand she has her degree in engineering but took this job because she couldn't find anyone willing to hire a woman engineer."

Abby took it as well as she could. "Beautiful?"

"Homely."

"Ah, that's too bad."

"Small, squat, swarthy, has a moustache."

"Now, now."

"I wouldn't fib about an unfortunate thing like that, truly I wouldn't."

"Then –"

"It's none of my business," Alice conceded, "but if you want to discuss the realities of life, I'm willing. Somehow or other, Mr. Norden deluded himself into thinking he could defeat Mr. Cleary on a battlefield of Mr. Cleary's

23

own choosing. Others have made that goof, and they're no longer employed by the company. I wonder why Mr. Norden made such a goof."

"I wouldn't know."

"If I were a woman in love with a hard-driving promotion specialist, I might be worried about him along about now."

"What else could I do?" Abby asked outright. "I help the man, and he climbs. I've been here three years. I've done about three hundred key papers for him. Bit by bit, he's climbed. When I came here, he was low man in the promotion department. He dreamed, I dreamed, and we worked together for what I thought was the common good. But now he has more dreams, and to get upstairs he needs a girl like Deanna Mikel."

"Quite a girl in any man's corner. Have you ever met her?"

"No."

"Stacked. Any bathing suit company that needs a model should get in touch with Miss Mikel. Also, she's impressive in street clothes. She has perfectly beautiful red hair and blue eyes. But the big thing to me is her creamy complexion."

"The big thing to Indigo, I'm afraid, is her last name."

A bell rang out front. Made restless by the

conversation and her melancholy thoughts, Abby went out front to answer. It was the vice president of designs himself, Mr. Cleary. Tall, spare, silver-haired, icy-eyed, Mr. Cleary nodded. "I'll have the schematics on our vacuum cleaner," he announced. "The Hurricane model that is."

Abby pressed the buzzer for Linda Aley. She got the call number from the card file and made out the requisition slip. Mr. Cleary signed with his gold fountain pen. After Linda had taken the slip off to the stack room, Mr. Cleary glanced around and then asked quietly: "What's this television antenna story, Miss Young? I've checked into the matter, naturally, and I can't see that it's such a top-flight project as Norden claims it is."

"It's the potential, I believe, Mr. Cleary."

"Oh, I've gathered that. But almost anything we become involved in has a potential if it works out. I have in my files right now, for example, plans for an electric stove that cooks with infra red and then browns meats and such electrically. All automatic, you understand. But plans are one thing, and a patentable invention is something else."

"Would you care to see the schematics and feasibility reports, sir, on the antenna?"

"Would you care to do Mr. Norden a favor, Miss Young?"

"Well . . ."

"You might inform that brash young man that our corporation exists to serve the public, not his personal ambition. Now I'm not opposed to him in the sense too many think I am. I actually admire him in many ways and for many reasons. But he's young, has much to learn, and is making a premature bid for a vice presidency. If I were a close friend of his, I'd advise him not to push it at this time. Others deserve first consideration. As a corporation man with a strong sense of loyalty to the workers who've built us up to our present position, I simply couldn't vote for him."

Abby felt, instinctively, that a dangerous pit was yawning directly ahead of her, a trap concealed not by grass or underbrush but by the blandest of little smiles. She looked down at her hands resting on the service counter. "Sir," she protested mildly, "should you be telling me these things? I know I like to think I'm important, but I'm just a librarian, after all. I don't think I should be involved in such matters."

"Miss Young, I have good reason to think you've authored certain important papers for Mr. Norden."

"Yes, sir. I've never made a secret of that. As I understand my position here, I'm to provide whatever research or abstract service employees want. But I've never written on administrative matters."

He was interested. He came around the counter and gestured for her to follow him into one of the private study rooms. He closed the door and motioned for her to sit at the table. He went to the small window and stood with hands clasped behind his back and a faint smile on his flattish, square-cut face. "A long time ago in Maine," he said quietly, "I learned to live and let live, Miss Young. We sons of Irish immigrant farmers did not have an easy time in those days, but we made life tolerable by adhering to that philosophy. I tell you this to underscore the fact I wish no person ill. I do what I must for the corporation that afforded me the opportunity to make something of myself. I have nothing against Norden but his youth and his opportunism. I have nothing against you if you satisfactorily perform the work you're paid to do. I'd resent it, as would the other vice presidents, if you ranged afield, as it were, to become involved in matters not properly your concern. There, does that clear the air between us?"

"Yes, sir. Thank you, sir."

He nodded. Perhaps his smile broadened a

27

bit, but the light made it difficult to tell. Certainly he spoke in a warmer tone when he said, "I myself find your work here most satisfactory, Miss Young. I was fearful, as were others, that you'd not work out. I felt, as did others, that a librarian with more experience ought to have been placed in this post. Still, it was difficult to ignore the recommendations of your professors and your predecessor here. As far as I'm concerned, you're the company's librarian for as long as you wish to be."

Abby heard Linda at the call desk. She got the report and handed it to Mr. Cleary. She was happy to notice that he at once began to read the abstract card clipped to the cover. The idea of providing abstracts with each report had been hers, it having been her theory that more often than not the technical people were interested in the essentials rather than details.

"We think we can improve this," Mr. Cleary said. "We have to. A Japanese firm has come out with a model much like this that can be manufactured for twelve dollars less and with no reduction in quality."

"Good heavens!"

His eyes brightened with the gleam of a natural-born fighter. "Competition's the stuff of life," he said zestfully. "I never enjoy myself, Miss Young, unless I have a business fight to wage."

He nodded and was gone, leaving Abby with considerable food for thought.

On Thursday, Alice came in just after lunch with still another tale to tell. Laughing, Alice said, "You must imagine a Norden confounded, Abby. That Rose Lovadero I mentioned on Tuesday will just have to endure the disappointment of not getting on Mr. Norden's list of girls to date and exploit."

"Thanks so much," Abby said testily.

Alice Hull colored and stirred uneasily. "I apologize," she said. "I'm just repeating what everyone around here says about the Norden technique for getting ahead."

"Why's he annoyed with Miss Lovadero? and stop looking so uneasy! I'd quit my job before I fired anyone, and you know it."

Alice smiled her relief. "The paper Rose wrote was a dog," Alice reported. "It read, I understand, like all those technical papers she writes for the brains in her department. Mr. Norden spent an hour looking up words in the dictionary and then quit."

Abby gloated; she couldn't help it.

"Mr. Norden did get an extension of the time they gave him to prepare the paper, though," Alice said. "The scoop I got is that he pleaded he had vital work on his desk. Now he's to present the paper on Monday."

"Let's spend the weekend in Boston, Alice."

Alice Hull's mouth formed a pert little O.

"If I'm away or tied up," Abby said frankly, "I won't weaken at the last moment."

"He hasn't come to you, has he?"

"He will."

"What on earth would we ever do in Boston?"

"Something exciting, I'm sure."

Alice spread her hands. "Well," she asked rhetorically, "who am I to say no?"

Indigo telephoned that same evening, as Abby had been sure he would. Again, she was "out." Friday afternoon, though, he invaded her office, as he had every right to. He slapped a briefcase on her desk. "I need an unbeatable paper by Sunday evening," he announced. "Now stop clowning around. You know better than to take all that girl talk seriously. You surprise me."

"No paper, Indigo. Sorry. That's administration stuff."

"Look!"

"Why should I?" Abby asked reasonably. "I could lose my job, and for what?"

"You know better than that."

"Sorry."

"Tough. Now we have to argue."

But Abby surprised herself, and him, by standing firm.

Chapter Four

At thirty, Indigo Norden was strapping and handsome proof that any man possessed of average intelligence, the killer instinct, and considerable self-confidence and drive could move fast and climb high even in a business area in which he'd had no basic training. When he was honest with himself, which was always, Indigo attributed his present lofty position to the silliness of women in general and young women in particular. The first job he'd ever gotten at Better Ways, Incorporated he owed to a comely auburn receptionist whom he still dated although she was no longer employed by the company. A flunky's job had been up for grabs in the promotion department of the company. In a large roomful of applicants, the receptionist had singled him out for a bright smile, which he'd returned. She'd then summoned him to her desk, briefed him on the right things to say to Mr. Eckert, and had sent him in first for an interview with the department chief.

Mr. Eckert had been immensely pleased by the clean-cut, well-spoken young man who seemed to have the correct views on all matters ranging from industry through religion and politics. It was doubtful that Mr. Eckert was as enthusiastic about Indigo Norden after an odd combination of events had compelled his early retirement. By then, naturally, it didn't matter what Mr. Eckert thought. Norden had his chair at the big desk in the department, and Norden always had been deaf to those who could do him no good or who wished him ill.

The initial job having been obtained, Indigo had spent several months making himself particularly useful to the oddest people: young women who functioned as technical typists and copywriters, young women who functioned as junior and senior secretaries, even young women who functioned as file clerks and office girls. One afternoon a rather cynical copywriter had informed Indigo, "There's no percentage in buttering up the skirts. In this place, Adam still rules." But Indigo's killer instinct had told him from the beginning that the flunky who buttered up the skirts could pick up from their owners more information about what was going on in the company than even the president ever got. His first promotion confirmed the wisdom of his policy of buttering up the skirts. Over Dutch-treat ice cream sodas with a junior secretary one evening, he'd learned that someone in promotion was nuts to use the wrong approach to selling a line of stainless steel potware to a national distributor. All Indigo's nerves sprang to the alert. But knowing women, he said a bit testily, "I'd rather talk about your eyes, if you don't mind." Pleased, she'd allowed him to discuss their wicked sparkle, the crisp delineation of the retina, the insouciant lashes. But bit by bit he'd gotten the information that the *correct* way to sell Mr. Bolz was to emphasize such technical matters as alloys, handle design, ease of washing and scouring, and so forth. A visit to the technical library had seemed in order, and there Indigo had met a slim, intense, earnest young thing who'd obviously devoted more time to books than to young fellows on the prod for success. Miss Abigail Henrietta Young. Would he ever forget the shock it had given him when he'd learned her full name?

Such a helpful Miss Young!

Armed with the results of her research, he'd dashed off a sales letter to Mr. Bolz. An order ... a beam from Mr. Eckert ... a promotion to the rank of junior copywriter.

Such a helpful Miss Young!

Armed with the results of her research and

inspirited by her shy, somewhat awkward kisses – so touching, really! – he'd moved up almost like a skyrocket. Then the major report to the president of the company himself, a quite overpowering two-hundred pager entitled: *Efficient Utilization of Promotion in an Era of Optimum Competition and Negative Reaction to Excessive Automation.* Miss Abigail Henrietta Young had indeed outdone herself. By thunder, the mere title alone had all but left Mr. Wente gasping for air! And every fact in the report was unassailable by Cleary and his cohorts! And every conclusion was drawn so skillfully from the unassailable facts that even Cleary had said during the final conference, "That report, Norden, is a goodie."

Such a helpful Miss Young!

She, of all people, had arranged the party in celebration of his promotion to department-head status and eighteen thousand a year. And if there was much kissing by the file clerks and the office girls, the technical typists and the copywriters, the junior and senior secretaries, so what? "Women are so emotional, you know, Abby."

A good-humored wag of the finger, a girlish admonition, "You behave, though!" a less shy and awkward kiss from her – and in public, yet! – and there, at thirty, he was.

Only in America, Indigo often said, could such things happen; only in America did dedicated effort and industry and know-how pay off. At the next meeting of his Kiwanis Club he even made a speech on that subject, a speech the members had applauded with gusto. . . .

But now things had changed.

That fact was much in Indigo's mind when he wakened around noon on the last Saturday in October. He lay smoking, thinking it over, until his stomach developed that queasy, nauseated condition his doctor attributed to too many cigarettes before breakfast. Indigo stubbed the third cigarette and hollered. After the fifth shout, Neumeyer came in briskly with a pot of coffee. "Breakfast in three shakes, sir," he said. "I trust we slept well?"

"We didn't. Too many girls capering and cheering around my grave. Do you know what the headstone carried for my epitaph? *Here lies all that remains of a lunkhead.* Neumeyer, remind me every morning from here on in not to trust women."

"Yes, sir."

"Blonde women in particular."

"Yes, sir."

"Miss Abigail Henrietta Young specifically."

"Yes, sir."

35

Indigo tried the coffee. "You can do better," he growled. "I don't expect much, Neumeyer, because I've been through the mill myself. But I do expect decent coffee. A man's entitled to something, isn't he?"

"Too strong, sir?"

"Neumeyer, my teeth rattled when I took that last sip. Any calls from Miss Young?"

"No, sir."

"Well, fix me some breakfast and then telephone Deanna Mikel. I'll go boating with her at one sharp. No, make that one-thirty. I hate to hurry breakfast."

"Yes, sir."

To his surprise, Indigo discovered under the shower that he wasn't angry with Abby Young or even especially worried about the forthcoming showdown on Monday. He liked the discovery. He held his hand straight out and bragged to himself, Nerves of steel. When you got right down to it, he thought, there was the real secret of his success. Never once in all his life had he doubted himself or panicked in any way in a tight situation. There'd been times when a lesser man would have. Last Wednesday, for instance, when he'd had to ask for more time and Cleary had sat with those icy eyes fixed on him and that smug smile on his face. But he'd wriggled out of the trap, all right, using the old brain every second of the time. So on Monday, if need be, he'd do some more wriggling. He'd get away with it, too, because he never panicked and never sold himself short.

At five minutes past one, Indigo got into his Chrysler convertible roadster and drove to Goose Point Bay. He found Deanna waiting impatiently in her Chris Craft cruiser. "A girl could freeze out here," she complained.

"It was your idea, I think. My idea of a perfect Saturday afternoon is you in my arms and an oak fire burning on the hearth. But I'm an easygoing guy. Any time a beautiful redhead asks me to indulge her, I'll be generous and indulge her."

Her eyes danced. "I could kiss you and kiss you," she said, "when you talk such nonsense. I know it's just a line. Don't ever think you can mislead me as you've misled those poor creatures at the office. Still, it's such a *nice* line."

"It's a relief to meet a girl I can't mislead," Indigo told her. "Do I kiss you hello now or later on?"

Very sternly she motioned for him to get aboard and sit on the port side of the cruiser. With beautiful athletic grace, she got the mooring lines untied and came leaping down again into the boat. An expert fiddling with levers and such got the motor to rumbling powerfully. She swung the boat around and sent it streaking into the bay. For about ten minutes all they did was sail bows on into one whitecap after another. Deanna cheered and whooped and squealed and laughed. She was wild, absolutely wild, with the thrill of hurtling to and fro at full throttle. Or was it, Indigo wondered sagaciously, a wilderness born and nurtured by good old female delight in a heap big conquest? Women, he reflected fondly, were such odd little dears. God had never made a homely woman and never would, and a fellow could no more resist womanly allure than he could resist food when hungry. Yet the little dears never seemed aware there was never a conquest involved; just things that had been ordained by their birth.

"Guess what?" he asked.

"What?"

"I'm having philosophic thoughts. You may not know it, but that's an insult to your pulchritude."

Her wildness ended, just like that. So happy a glow lit her eyes it shamed him to be with her and to be that important to her. "Unlax," he said gently. "I'm just a guy. You may not believe it, but I have my flaws."

"Name one."

"Stupidity."

"Really? How cute!"

Indigo went to work, his killer instinct telling him now was the time to dispose of the Monday problem.

"But I am stupid, I'm afraid. I relied on Abby Young to do an important research job for me. I have to get a report to the powers that be on Monday. Well, Abby decided to be inordinately jealous of you. And to teach me a lesson, I suppose, she took off for Boston and left me in the lurch."

Deanna stopped the engine. At once, the boat began to rock and toss on the incoming tidal swells. Indigo thought of protesting, but decided not to. He liked the shrewd, angry gleam in those gorgeous blue eyes. A shrewd and angry woman, he knew, could always figure out at least one or two useful angles.

"It grabs me," Deanna said, "to know that there are resentful Communists in Daddy's company. I think I'll have to tell Daddy about Miss Young."

Indigo swallowed hard. Indigo shook his head.

"Well, it was an idea," Deanna said. "You remember it if you ever have to dispose of Miss Young. I could tell Daddy I took up so much of your time this weekend you never did get a chance to think about that silly report."

Indigo considered the suggestion. There

39

was one major thing wrong with it. He could hardly give all his weekend to Deanna for the good and simple reason he had a date with Grace that evening, a date with Helen tomorrow morning, and a date with Elaine tomorrow afternoon and evening. How could he explain the gorgeous redhead to those girls if he showed up for the different dates with Deanna clinging to his arm?

"I think not," he said. "I don't want to use our friendship in a business way. I know you'll find this incredible, your beauty considered, but your friendship happens to be precious to me."

"How precious?"

"Precious."

Deanna slid over to his side of the boat. Enchanting in her heavy levis and gay turtleneck sweater, she closed her eyes and unabashedly turned up her face for a kiss. Her lips were warm, soft, and tasted faintly of sea brine.

"Isn't it odd," Deanna asked, opening her eyes, "how people change as they age? I never was known in college as a girl who liked to park with a fellow under the moon. I don't mind parking with you, though, even under the sun. May I do you a kindness?"

"Not if it's involved with business."

"Silly boy. Anything that worries you

worries me, so it's my business, not yours. Now, then, what do we do all day today and all day tomorrow?"

"Hang it, Deanna, it just happens I have some business engagements I can't break."

Her nose crinkled becomingly as she asked, "Care to bet?"

Giving in, as he had to, Indigo consoled himself with the thought it was really a small price, a trifling price, to pay for a clear shot at a vice presidency.

Chapter Five

Snow was falling when Abby Young went down to breakfast in Washburn House on Monday morning. Colonel Delaney and young Sally Washburn were already at the small round table. The table had been shifted nearer the windows so that the early diners could enjoy the spectacle without having to crane. Sally's pudgy face was pink with delight and excitement. "I just adore snow!" she exclaimed. "I hate every season except winter."

"This is still autumn," Abby reminded her. She pretended not to see the colonel's murderous glance. "I understand," she went on, "that you're looking for part-time work."

"Well, Mom thinks I should do something. I personally think that if I concentrate on school and my social activities, I'll be doing more than enough. But Mom thinks it's time I showed more ambition."

"We have to make a beginning," Colonel Delaney cut in briskly. He fixed his single brown eye on the young face. He said sternly, "When I was your age, I was already a modest businessman. I had my own newspaper route."

"Really? I definitely thought you never worked for anyone but the Army."

"Beginnings are beginnings, Washburn. I'd play up to Miss Young, if I were you. You'd be lucky indeed if she got you a beginning in Better Ways, Incorporated. A sound business establishment. I know. I own a hundred shares of its preferred stock."

Mrs. Kurzen came in with boiled eggs for the colonel and Sally and oatmeal for Abby. Cracking an egg open, Sally asked somewhat fearfully, "What kind of job did you have in mind for me, Miss Young? I got to talking to that pretty Mr. Ballantine yesterday, and he told me to hold out for work on the call desk."

"Did he, now!"

"Not that I want a job, frankly," Sally said.

"I'd take one just to please Mom and you."

Colonel Delaney had difficulty with his throat at that point. He coughed, he sputtered, he coughed some more. Recourse to water helped only until Sally added as an afterthought, "But you'd have to pay me a minimum of two dollars an hour. A laborer is worthy of his hire. I read that somewhere." A veritable paroxysm of coughing finally silenced Sally.

"The job I thought I might give you, dear," Abby said, "is sort of an errand girl's job in the stacks. The pay would be forty cents an hour for three hours an afternoon five days a week."

"Well, there you are," Sally said to Colonel Delaney triumphantly. "I looked for work, but I couldn't find anything suitable."

After bacon and eggs and two slices of toast and a two-cup pot of coffee, Abby walked off through the snowstorm to work. She found it a bit tricky to cross Goose Point Bridge on foot, but she managed to get to her office a few minutes early and with minimum wear and tear. She got her coat hung and brushed, put on the old shoes she wore at work and went out to the employees' lounge. Alice Hull and Linda Aley were just getting into their smocks, and Sue Quentin came scooting in to punch the time clock with just two or three minutes to spare. "Lots of gossip in the cafeteria," Sue reported. "I was talking to Mr. Norden's secretary, and she said there'll be a lot of unhappy folks in the exec suite this morning."

"I wonder why?" Alice asked innocently.

"Well, according to Harriet, a lot of people seemed to think that Mr. Norden —"

But the bell was rung smartly up front. Abby went to the counter to handle the first patron of the week. She promptly wished she'd not. It was Indigo's secretary, and Harriet was smiling smugly. "Mr. Norden thought you should abstract and file this report at once," Harriet announced. "Mr. Mikel read it at breakfast this morning and said it represented some of the clearest thinking in years at Better Ways, Incorporated."

Abby glanced at the title. She winced, wondering who on earth he'd found at the last minute to write a report called: *Theories on the Protection of Potentially Profitable Ideas.* "My," she said heartily, "I'm glad someone got around to writing on that subject. There's a definite need for guidance by some authority."

"Well, that's what Mr. Mikel said, as a matter of fact. Mr. Norden said he'd be glad to do more such things if ever he got the rank you need to make people pay attention to what you write. They'll be reading a copy of this report in the exec suite this morning."

"Grand."

"Mr. Norden thought you'd like to hear about it, Miss Young. That's why he sent me here right off."

But even worse was to come.

Around eleven o'clock, Linda Aley brought a beautiful redhead into the office and said most respectfully, "This is Miss Young, our head librarian, Miss Mikel. Miss Young, Miss Mikel."

Abby contrived a smile. "I'm so happy to meet you, Miss Mikel," she fibbed, rising. "Your father has mentioned you from time to time, but he never told me how lovely you are. Won't you sit down?"

But first Miss Mikel had to be helped with her sassy mink hat and full-length mink coat. Linda performed the service almost reverently. "I'll have coffee," Miss Mikel announced, and Linda fetched a cupful quicker than Abby had ever dreamed was possible. When all had been seen to and Miss Mikel was quite comfortable, Miss Mikel favored Abby with a twinkling glance. "You've seen Indigo's report by now, I dare say?" she asked. "It was so unfortunate you had to visit Boston. It took almost ten minutes of my time to arrange ghost-writing service for Indigo."

Abby said carefully, "I've seen the report, Miss Mikel."

"And have read it for goofs?"

"That isn't my function, Miss Mikel. I'm afraid Mr. Norden gave you the wrong impression of the work I do here. I read professional papers and journals and order copies of things I think may be useful to our technical and scientific and administrative people. I order and shelve books related to our work. I supervise the provision of reference, bibliographic, circulation, and photostatic services to all personnel. Last, but definitely not least, I file and abstract all professional reports written by our personnel. But I *don't*, Miss Mikel, review any report for technical accuracy."

"How many goofs did you find?"

"Would, you like sugar and powdered cream, Miss Mikel?"

"I drink coffee black. I'm that sort of person, Miss Young. No fuss, no bother. I drink coffee black, I smoke unfiltered cigarettes, I chase after the men who amuse me, I hound my enemies, and I ask direct questions to which I expect direct answers."

To Abby, the disconcerting thing was that it all had been said by sweetly smiling lips. She

46

couldn't help but recall the sweet smile that had accompanied the thief's threat last week to kick the detective's teeth down his throat.

"To repeat, Miss Young, how many goofs did you find?"

Abby got the point then. Miss Mikel's objective wasn't to gloat but to scare, and not so much to scare as to squash an adversary under the weight of her position.

It took an effort, but Abby managed to respond pleasantly. "I'm afraid you're not authorized to ask questions of me, Miss Mikel. Corporation policy is to provide information only to those authorized to receive it."

"I see."

Miss Mikel sipped the coffee. She then leaned forward a bit tensely and said, "I can appreciate your resentment of me, Miss Young. You perhaps were encouraged by Indigo's behavior to imagine he was more serious than he was. But that's not the case in point just now. I have a brilliant father. From time to time he talks to me about business and the ways of the business world, and I listen. One thing he told me made quite an impression on me. He said, and I quote him: 'To fight a war, you need an army.' I think that's singularly apropos here."

"I wasn't aware I was fighting a war, Miss Mikel."

"I've decided, Miss Young, that poor Indigo deserves a promotion to staff. All other heads of key departments are vice presidents, and I believe that the promotion department is a key department. Now don't you think it would be unrealistic of you to displease a man headed for a vice presidency?"

"I try to displease no one, Miss Mikel."

"Fine. And so, by that roundabout route, we return to my original question. That was: how many goofs did you find?"

"I'm sorry, Mikel, but policy is policy. I believe your father established the policy, by the way."

Smiles stopped.

The little dimpled chin came forward.

The beautiful eyes flashed.

Before Miss Mikel could storm, however, Mr. Cleary came in quite jauntily, dapper and austere in a pearl gray suit. He tossed a report onto Abby's desk. "I found this interesting, Miss Young," he said. "Some gibberish or other authored by Norden."

"Mr Cleary!"

Mr. Cleary smiled at Miss Mikel. "Well, now, Deanna," he said, "you mustn't glower at me that way. I expressed the considered opinion of the staff."

"Mr. Cleary," Abby said, "Miss Mikel wants to know how many goofs I found in Mr. Norden's latest report. I told her about corporation policy regulating the provision of information to authorized people only. I'm afraid I offended her without wishing to."

"Can't be done," Mr. Clearly said promptly. "If our librarian didn't adhere to that policy, Deanna, she'd be out of work in three days."

"My father does happen to be executive vice president, I believe."

"Now I've heard that, too," Mr. Cleary admitted. He thought things over and then came up with a happy idea. "Why," he said, "it's just occurred to me, Miss Young, that there's no justification now for refusing to answer the question. The report has been rejected. Therefore, it isn't company information that has to be guarded. How many errors of fact and thought did you find? I'm curious to know if your tally agrees with mine."

Abby looked at Miss Mikel and said gently, "I'd reached two hundred errors when I stopped reading."

"I found three hundred and sixty-two," Mr. Cleary announced.

The beautiful redhead just sat there a moment, all but stunned.

To give her time to recover, Abby looked up at Mr. Cleary and said, "Basically, though, sir, Mr. Norden's position on the matter is correct."

"These days," he said sarcastically, "everyone's an officer of the corporation."

"Sir, if the information on the electronic television antenna is publicized in open court, we run two risks. We risk giving valuable information about the antenna to a competitor, and we risk tipping off our competitors to the general direction some of our work is taking."

His eyes narrowed. "It seems odd to me," he said quite respectfully, "that you never got into business administration, Miss Young. You have, I've noticed, a flair for getting to the essence of things. All your abstracts indicate that, and various papers you've – well, er – edited for Mr. Norden."

"I love being a technical librarian, sir."

"Then we're doubly fortunate, because we have an able technical librarian and a happy employee. Well, to relieve your mind, Miss Young, let me say that the antenna papers have been classified 'secret,' and the proper court has been so informed."

Miss Mikel recovered magnificently. "Then why on earth do you call that report gibberish?" she asked.

Mr. Cleary shrugged. "His argument was based entirely on technical reasons. The real reason the work ought not to be publicized is that, as Miss Young has just said, we don't want to tip off our competitors to the general direction our work here is taking."

An interesting idea occurred to Mr. Cleary.

"Miss Young," he ordered, "do a report on the subject, will you? It would please me to bring your sound thinking to the attention of our staff."

Mr. Cleary smiled and bowed and left. Miss Mikel went to the costumer for her mink coat and mink hat. "I'm afraid," Miss Mikel said, "that we're at war, Miss Young. I'm sorry. I find such things a dreadful bore."

Chapter Six

Told, Chet Ballantine expressed concern. "I know Norden's type," he said worriedly, "as I've mentioned before. If he thinks he has a reasonable chance to make a vice presidency, he'll go all out for the promotion. And if he thinks for some reason or other that you're a threat to his chance, he'll go for your jugular vein."

51

They were having their customary Tuesday evening Italian dinner in Scopazzi's on Front Street. In the glare of fluorescent lights, the piled up snow along the sidewalk had a sickly color. Few pedestrians could be seen. Traffic was minimal. The first snow of the season having come, it seemed reluctant to stop coming. Abby could see in the fluorescent glare great puffs of flakes floating down steadily, almost purposefully. She supposed that to the hundreds of unemployed engaged to clean the streets of Cantwell, the snowfall seemed truly manna from heaven. Only thought of those people getting needed work prevented her from wishing the snow would stop. A memory impelled her to ask the waiter for another bowl of minestrone soup. Catching Chet looking at her in surprise, she explained, "Sometimes, as a child, I went hungry. One year my father got work in New York on the business end of a snow shovel. He came home with a roast, a fine, tender, juicy roast. Mother scolded him for his extravagance, but the hotel people he'd shoveled snow for had given him the roast as a bonus. I could have eaten that roast raw. My mouth watered and my stomach ached as I sat in the kitchen waiting for the roast to finish cooking. I ate and I ate and I ate. I vomited it all up later on, of course, but I still remember that roast on snowy nights when I think of all the unemployed getting a few dollars for shoveling snow."

Chet reached across the table and squeezed her hand. It was odd, but that quick hand squeeze told her much about Chet. Deep down, the guy was more emotional than he liked people to think.

When the soup had been brought, Abby sprinkled Parmesan cheese over it liberally. "You have more, too," she urged. "Oh, and this dinner is on me."

"I wouldn't think of it."

"It's nice to be able to afford to treat someone to dinner, Chet. And I'm celebrating something."

"What?"

"The discovery that I don't scare easily, the discovery that my principles, such as they are, mean a great deal to me."

"If we'd been drinking wine, Abby, I'd suspect you'd had a glass too much."

Simply smelling the thick, savory soup thrilled Abby. The taste gave her exquisite pleasure. As she sometimes did when gloriously happy, she waxed a trifle silly. "A bowl of soup and thou," she teased; "why wouldn't I be intoxicated?"

He smiled gently. "You gorge and I'll watch," he suggested. "I'd like to think about the Norden thing a bit more before I give you advice."

"Why would I need advice? Chet, you ninny, I was telling you much more than a ghastly tale of poverty when I told you about the roast. I was really telling you that Indigo and I have one thing in common: we'll both battle very, very hard to keep what we have or to get ahead. And it isn't an uneven war, if war it's to be. I came well recommended, I've done a top job, I'm not without friends in the stratosphere."

"And you wouldn't be overconfident, would you?"

"Never! It's a fatal blunder, and don't you ever forget it! I just don't think I'm entirely helpless, that's all."

"He's a wheel, I have to remind you."

"I never forget that," Abby assured him. "Believe me, Chet, I never forget that."

After dinner he wanted to escort her home, but she talked him out of the idea, because she knew that once he'd gotten comfortably seated in the boarding house living room, he'd stay until Mrs. Washburn pointedly said, "I *always* lock up at two in the morning." Chet was all right. When you could extricate him from the various work traps he created for himself, he could be excellent company. But there was a time for all the joys of peace, and there was a time for war. This, unless she missed her guess, was a time for war. So, of course, first things had to be put first – such things as banging out that report Mr. Cleary had asked her to write.

That evening, despite her heavy dinner, Abby found her brain functioning like a fine watch. Within an hour after she'd settled down at her desk, she'd pulled all her ideas since Monday morning into a rough outline. Two hours later she had a detailed and polished outline. Moreover, she thought contentedly, she had an outline for a *fine* report. The next two days, whenever she could take time from library work, she researched the material she wanted to include in the report. It seemed to her that the most effective way to put her basic theme across was to cite the records of actual articles and gadgets the corporation had developed and marketed down through the years. She chose the Better Ways vacuum cleaner, the Better Ways electric floor brush, the Better Ways hearing aid, the Better Ways floor and car wax, and the Better Ways "Be a Millionaire" parlor game. By dint of considerable research, she got together all the material she could possibly assemble on development costs, manufacturing costs, and total profits down through the years. Then, armed with her outline and unassailable facts, she sat down to write a paper entitled: *On the Economic Necessity to Conserve Theoretical and Demonstrated Knowledge for the Benefit of the Stockholders*. She loved the title. The title was wordy enough to please Mr. Wente, it was stuffy enough to please Mr. Cleary, and it was practical enough to please the vice presidents of finance, manufacture and sales.

The writing required seven long evenings. It was a bitter grind, for despite Indigo's thoughts to the contrary, composition had never come easily to her. Then, too, she was painfully aware that Indigo and his supporters would do their dead-level best to pick the thing apart. The awareness made her jumpy, self-conscious, uncertain. Still, bit by bit she got the first draft finished. Knowing no one else to test it on, she gave it to Chet for a preliminary analysis.

Three days elapsed before Chet gave her his views. On the first day, Friday, at eleven o'clock, she got her first reward for her persistent industry. Indigo came in unannounced and without knocking, his shock of blue-black hair disheveled, his fine gray eyes twinkling with irrepressible verve – and worry! "Let's talk," he said, taking a chair. "My little black book isn't the same without you."

"Hi, Indigo! Or do I call you Mr. Norden now?"

"Not yet, not yet. These things slow down a bit when you near the top. The skyrocket meets more resistance, which is a statement that would probably startle a fellow like Chet Ballantine. But you know what I mean, I guess."

"I know what you mean."

"What did you think of Deanna?"

"Beautiful."

"Oh, that? Honey, I can make with the line as well as any man I know, but I kid you not when I say that for real beauty, I'll take you over her any day of the week. She's a girl; you're a woman. There's a great big difference there, believe me."

Abby was just silly enough to feel pleased. "I must say," she said breathily, "that I admire your taste in women."

Indigo leaned back and roared with laughter. He sputtered, "Don't ever change. Don't you ever change!"

Annoyed with her emotions, Abby said more briskly, "I'm really rather busy, Indigo."

"Doing what?" he challenged.

"Indigo, we have perhaps fifteen thousand volumes in the stacks and perhaps forty thousand reports in our reports section. I have a problem I never solve: what books to keep; what books to dispose of to make room for newer, more up-to-date material. And the reports! I abstract. I cross-file. I have them put on film. I have them put on tape. And all this isn't enough. We received a suggestion the other day that we circulate throughout the building a weekly paper that summarizes *all* the reports issued during the week."

He wagged his head. "I'll never understand, Abby, why these guys have to do so much reading. They all went to colleges or universities, didn't they? Didn't they learn anything except how to read and do mathematics? Can't they spend all the reading time on work that'll make money for the corporation?"

Abby thought the least said the better; therefore she said nothing.

"We have a twenty-story building here," Indigo went on, building up a head of steam, "and on all the floors except one we have hundreds of men and women who are supposed to ransack their brains for ideas for products that'll bring the moola rolling in. Do you know how many ideas that whole gang came up with last year?"

"Twelve, I believe."

"Twelve! Think of that! Hundreds of

brainy men and women drawing fat pay checks, and they come up with twelve ideas in a whole year!"

"And perhaps forty ideas for improving products in the market, Indigo."

"Rah, rah, rah, college!"

"Each of those twelve new ideas, Indigo, will bring in millions of dollars in profit annually for the next five or six years. The other forty will account for many more millions in profits. Now I'd like to say something in defense of the technical and scientific personnel here. Better still, I'll quote something one of the inventors here once said. He said that all of us in support services, meaning you and meaning me, Indigo, are really riding on the shoulders of the technical and scientific people."

Indigo went white. "That's a dirty lie!"

"Well, Indigo, I know I never bring in a dollar of profit for the company. How many dollars of profit do you bring in?"

"We promote these things. We sell them to the public or Uncle Sam."

"Not really. The products are useful, necessary, so they're bought. Without the products, where are you and where am I?"

He began to breathe stertorously. She'd never seen him so angry. She began to wonder if deep down Indigo didn't sometimes wonder just how essential he was to Better Ways, Incorporated.

He stopped her wandering mind short by saying, "Chet Ballantine made that crack, Abby. Don't kid me. He's had his hooks in us more than once."

"The point is –"

"The point is we have a big, smooth, profitable organization, Abby. The point is that anyone who throws or tries to throw that kind of monkey-wrench into the machinery isn't worth having around. The point is I know you're working with Chet Ballantine on that stupid report, and I don't like having a man with his attitude involved in this thing between us."

Abby said, "I didn't declare war, Indigo. Until she made the declaration, I didn't even know that Miss Mikel fancied herself in the role of a general."

"I want to see the report before Cleary sees it."

"What? Why, I couldn't do that."

He aimed a forefinger at her as if he thought it a cannon. "Or we are at war, Abby, and I'll have you out on your ear one way or another. I have a shot at the great big exec suite, and I'm not going to miss or be made to miss."

"Now wait a minute, Indigo! You put me

into this predicament, and you know it. I had a right to go to Boston, I had a right to refuse extra work at no pay. You couldn't let well enough alone. For once, just for once, one of your infatuated women refused to roll over and play dead. You couldn't tolerate that. Your ego wouldn't permit it. So enter General Deanna Mikel to battle for you as you've had women battle for you all through the years. Very well, I happen to know something about fighting, too, and I promise you this: I promise, Indigo, that before I'm eased out on my ear, as you so graciously expressed it, you'll regret you ever started any of this."

"Do I or don't I see the report?"

"Mr. Norden, you don't. That's work done on my own time at the request of a staff member named Mr. Cleary. I don't have to show it to you, and I won't."

"I'll call off the battle here and now if I can look at that report."

"No, sir."

She had the reward of seeing him look extremely worried just before he left. And on Monday, when Chet finally told her, "Submit as is; it can't be argued down," she had her second reward for her industry. There was new respect in Chet Ballantine's brown eyes, by golly.

But the finest reward of all came late that

Monday afternoon. Mr. Cleary telephoned and said: "Excellent." He didn't have to say more. Score the first victory in the war, Abby exulted, for General Young!

Chapter Seven

On November eighteenth, Abby had the interesting experience of being sat down in the technical information department by Better Ways, Incorporated, for interrogation by a technical editor on certain matters involved in the publication of her report. The editor was a short, squat, swarthy woman who had an almost embarrassing facsimile of a black moustache. "Rose Lovadero," the woman introduced herself. She didn't miss the sudden gleam in Abby's eyes. "The technical writer who goofed," she admitted. "In my own defense, I suppose I should say I wasn't too well briefed. This is a sound report, Miss Young. I wish I'd written it."

"Thank you."

"Do you have an engineer's training, Miss Young?"

"No. I'm familiar with the terminology, of course, and I suppose I do understand some technical matters in the broad sense of the word."

"I like your introduction, Miss Young. It's the finest justification I've yet read for all the money the corporation is investing in research and development. I don't think there's any harm in telling you that it's planned to send a copy of that introduction to every stockholder in the company."

Modesty dictated some disclaimer or other, but Abby was too thrilled to bring off the pretense. Miss Lovadero grinned sympathetically. "I know how you feel," she confided. "I practically popped my buttons when I received my first commendation. I have only a few changes to suggest in the report, by the way. Some are editorial changes such as headings. I could do that for you, if you wish."

"By all means."

"The other change, Miss Young, concerns certain conclusions you derived from the sales record of the electric floor sweeper. The conclusions aren't quite valid, because you neglected to take into account the fact that some of the sales resulted from extremely costly promotion from coast to coast. If you deduct the cost of this promotion from the profits you list, then the sweeper isn't quite the hot shot you say it was."

"Change it, then."

Miss Lovadero nodded. "I think it would be wise. Off the record, Miss Young, I have to give you some perhaps painful news. On December first, when this report comes out, you'll be identified permanently with the technical and scientific group in this establishment. Administrators and strictly business people will be arrayed against you. You can be sure they'll examine your figures with a microscope to catch you in damaging errors."

"Well . . ."

"You see, Miss Young, there are two factions in Better Ways, Incorporated. One faction would like to downgrade the technicians and scientists. Why? Simple. If so much credit is due to them, then fatter salaries should be paid the inventors and developers rather than the administrators and other business people. That faction, I'm sorry to report, appears to be rallying around Mr. Norden."

"How can I be in either camp? I serve everyone here. I was ordered to write a report, and I wrote one."

"The other faction, the one I'll call the scientific faction, will naturally make much of your report. Since I belong to that faction, I want to be sure no errors can be spotted."

Abby stood up, not liking the idea of seeming to be a member of any faction. "Well, do whatever you wish with the report," she said. "Frankly, I never expected it to be published."

"I know, Miss Young. I also know that Mr. Norden didn't expect publication, either. This is an interesting corporation to work for, I find. Rank counts for little; results or accomplishments count for everything. I just may apply for work as an engineer one of these days to ascertain the company's attitude on female engineers."

Both thrilled and disturbed, Abby hurried back to her office and passed the news along to Alice Hull. Alice quirked her brows. "I'd not be disturbed," Alice said. "The upper echelon must know you were assigned the job. No one can accuse you of having sneaked in something to make a big splash."

"If I were in Indigo's position, Alice, I'd make the accusation anyway. Enough people will believe him, because they'll want to believe him."

"How can a nice girl like you think such things as that?"

But Indigo Norden, it developed, could be as subtle as a chessmaster when he thought it worth-while to make the effort. On publication day, Indigo came into the office and said, "Author ! Author! I demand your autograph!"

Abby waited.

Indigo closed the door with a backward flip of his left foot. "I'll say this for you," he said. "When you kill an argument, you kill it dead."

"Thanks, Indigo."

"Last time I was here, doll baby, I made some threats. I was angry, jumpy, you know how it is? I've been thinking it over. Okay, I can look at our scrap from your point of view. You've always craved five children, a proper home, reasonable security, community position and respect. You looked at Indigo and decided all this was possible and even probable through him. Indigo let you down, or so you thought. Right?"

"Right."

"Well, there you are. Indigo can't help being Indigo. You know that or ought to know. He has a burning passion to get ahead. He has a burning passion to be Mr. Big to girls. Kid stuff? Yup, could be. But a man is what he is, period. All right. After Deanna, there'll be the push to exec vice president and then the big chair. But you don't have to figure in any of this. I hurt you, you hurt me, and right now we're even. You can have this job for the rest of your life, and an even better one, perhaps, if you call it quits now. How's about it?"

Abby surprised in those fine gray eyes a sentiment that moved her profoundly. Why, the big, hard-driving, amoral character was sincerely offering her a way out that would preserve her dignity and self-respect!

"Why does it have to be this way?" she asked. "We're happy when we're together. You've said that a hundred times."

"If I had a million in my pocket, I'd marry you yesterday," Indigo said. "Does that answer your question?"

"Listen —"

But he was moving toward the door with powerful, long-legged strides. "I'll forget the report," he said magnanimously. "I can't forget Chet's crack about me or the help he gave you, natch, but I'll forget the report."

"I may marry Chet, Indigo."

It was as if she'd never spoken. Striking a fist into his right palm, he said feverishly, "I have to make a splash, a great big splash." He went out and slammed the door behind him.

Hugely disturbed now, Abby did something she'd not done before: she telephoned Chet in the Development Lab on the eighteenth floor. He came downstairs quickly and sat impassively while he heard her out. "I can't fret about Norden," Chet then said calmly. "I do my work, he does his, we seldom meet."

"Chet, is there any way he could use you to make what he calls a big splash?"

He smiled amusedly. "If so, I'm more important around here than I ever thought."

"How important are you?"

His brown eyebrows lifted, then lowered. "Hard to answer objectively, I'm afraid. I've worked on many projects, including most of those you mentioned in that report. We market a special wrench I designed and perfected, a nice money-maker for the company. There are other things – nothing spectacular, mind, but steady money-makers. I have two or three basic patents, as far as that goes."

"What does that mean?"

"You'd have to get a legal expert to figure it out. I work on contract around here."

It baffled Abby. Judging from the things Chet was saying, there was little, if anything, to distinguish him from all the others who expended brain power in the corporation's behalf. What good would it do Indigo to use Chet to make a big splash? Apart from a few people in the place, it was doubtful anyone really knew of Chet's existence. Yet twice Indigo had singled Chet out for a blast. Why?

That same evening, Colonel Ned Delaney seemed to find it no mystery at all, though. Arms resting on his knees, Colonel Delaney looked toward the crackling fire and said, "Diversionary tactics, Miss Young. Has Norden had officers' training? Routine action, really. Often, to make a frontal assault over difficult ground, you make a diversionary attack at the far end of your line. If the diversionary attack is launched in strength, the enemy must direct his fire at it, concentrate his attention upon it. Then when your frontal attack begins, he opposes it with less strength than he had in the beginning. I imagine Norden wants to divert your attention in some way or other."

Abby sighed. "I don't understand that, either," she confessed. "I'm not an enemy intent upon defeating Indigo Norden. I just grew weary of doing so much for him in exchange for promises he had no intention of making good. I wrote a report that embarrassed him a trifle, but he knows I was ordered to write it."

His good eye flicked to her face. He pushed his lips in and out two or three times while he studied her. A quiet-faced man with grizzled hair and a massive chin and jaw, he finally asked, "Are you sure you're not a problem to him in one way or another? I had an officer in France who was unwittingly a problem to another officer. Things were touch and go for a time."

"Sir, how could I be? I earn nine thousand a year as head librarian. If I'm very fortunate I might get up to twelve thousand a year in another twenty or thirty years. Right now, Indigo Norden earns eighteen thousand a year for doing an excellent, even a brilliant job as promotions director for the corporation. It isn't at all unlikely that he'll be a vice president in a year or so. His youth considered, he has an excellent chance to become president of the corporation one of these years."

"No."

"No?"

"I've met important businessmen in my time, young lady. All of them had one thing in common: a rare talent for concentrating only upon the important. If your Mr. Norden is wasting his time on a vendetta involving you or Mr. Ballantine or both, then he doesn't have what it takes to be a corporation president. And that lack of basic ability, of perception, of judgment, will be the undoing of his hopes. In my military experience I discovered early that men, like water, seek and find their natural level. This man can climb just so high, another man can climb just a notch above him, and so forth. I call it the inexorable law of competency."

"Well, he's personally involved with me, you see. And Chet – well, Chet's been a friend a long time, too."

"I'd not be diverted by any move in Mr. Ballantine's direction, Miss Young. Now, then, I'd like to discuss young Sally Washburn with you."

"Sir, you heard me offer her work. And I did that only as a courtesy to you. I can't beg a girl her age to come work for me. There'd be no discipline if she believed she was doing me a favor."

"I've discussed the matter with her half-sister. June's been urging Sally to take the post. I think that if you had a woman-to-woman chat with that child, she'd be inclined to do some serious thinking."

"Right now, sir, if I had a woman-to-woman chat with any girl, I'd urge her to grab her man while he still felt he needed her. I'm in a cynical and bitter mood these days."

"Seventeen's a critical age, Miss Young."

And so it was, Abby thought, but so was any other year in the life of an unmarried but still yearning woman. Still, she thought, who was she to refuse anyone a helping hand? She nodded to Colonel Delaney and went up to Sally's room on the second floor. She found

71

Sally lying on her stomach in the middle of the floor, listening to a rock and roll record. Sally sat up and crossed her legs Turk fashion. "I definitely adore that music," Sally confided. "It makes me think about men. I adore thinking about men, don't you?"

"Sally, let's talk about life and jobs and fellows, shall we?"

The girl giggled. Promptly, she shut off the record player. "Let's begin with Adam," she urged. "All else is so atrociously dull."

Chapter Eight

An odd thing happened to Chet Ballantine on December fourth, and it wasn't until later, much later, that he appreciated its significance. Someone punched his doorbell while he was making his breakfast in his small, white-frame house in the Plymouth District of Cantwell. Chet opened up, thinking it might be Abby. He would have closed the door, knowing Deanna Mikel's reputation, but her right foot was quicker than his right hand. "Naughty, naughty, naughty," she said, stepping in. "I don't understand you, Chet. You're handsome, you're intelligent, you dance beautifully, you want to get ahead. You have everything going for you except the big thing: common sense."

"Want breakfast?"

"Buttermilk pancakes?"

"I'm that way," he said sheepishly. "If I like a thing, I like it. And I'm a man of habit, too, I suppose."

"The pancakes won't buy you anything," she warned. "I'm the same old Deanna. I have to be honest."

"It's agreed," he joked, "that the pancakes won't buy me anything except the charm of your company at breakfast."

He took her to the kitchen. She stopped in the doorway and looked around the kitchen with touching wistfulness. Her glance lingered on the stove, the refrigerator, the cupboards, the pot rack, the copper-bottomed potware, the round dinette table, the German cuckoo clock. "I'm glad everything's the same," she said simply. "I wondered. Some of the happiest hours of my life were spent in this kitchen."

"Glad to hear that, Deanna. What ever happened to the dream of becoming a great chef? The way you used to take over this place and practice . . . well, I thought you'd keep on and get somewhere."

"Father thought it unsuitable."

"And you must suit your father in these matters?"

She sat on one of the chairs, tucking one leg up under her. Her eyes danced vivaciously. "Ah," she begged, "let's not be too serious before breakfast. Will any of your neighbors be scandalized by my early visit? I could sit on the porch and freeze to death most respectably there."

He went over and gave her lovely nose a tweak.

"I'll have eight little pigs and five pancakes," she said greedily. "Don't bother about coffee for me. I drink milk these days. I find I don't need the stimulus of coffee as all the others in my family do."

Chet got the things from the refrigerator. He went to work on the batter, folding the ingredients in rather than beating them. "Always fold, never beat," he told her, "when you make buttermilk pancakes. A beaten batter makes a tough pancake."

"Uh-huh. Chet, may I ask a question and get an honest answer?"

"Yes."

"What happened to us, Chet? I've often wondered. I mean, why weren't you good enough for me? Why did I have to see magic in Tony, magic in Al, magic in so many, many fellows?"

"Simple. Beautiful thoroughbred race horses can't run with Dobbins."

She sucked air. Rapture brought a rich inner glow to her lovely face. "Chet," she said ecstatically, "that's the sweetest thing anyone's ever said to me!"

"Oh, I'm good at saying sweet things to women. It's among my many talents, that expertise."

"I'll tell you this, Chet. I know perfectly well that you're much too good for me. I sincerely mean that, Chet."

It gave him cause for deep thought, which occupied him while he made the breakfast. Her words made him uneasy because, coming from her, they were incongruous. A full year of his life had been devoted to what he had more than once called the Deanna Mikel phase of his existence. In that year he had seen her just about every evening and most of every weekend. His vacation had been spent there in Cantwell, because she had conceived the ridiculous project of exploring every inch of the waterfront of Cantwell and the adjacent rural area. So during the Deanna phase of his existence, he'd acquired a rather deep knowledge of her character and temperament. He'd learned early in the phase that when she was good she was very, very good, and when she was bad she was horrid. Also, he'd learned

75

that when she was finished with a fellow, she was truly finished with him, savagely so if he pestered her after her interest in him had ended. Then why was she with him this Sunday morning? It was odd. All the talk about his so-called merits as a man was just so much talk. He could see that in her eyes, in the cold depths that seemed to be appraising the effect of her every flattering word. What did she hope to accomplish with the talk?

The deep thought produced no answers to these vital questions.

Then, while they were eating breakfast, things happened fast.

First, the telephone rang.

It was the executive vice president of Better Ways, Incorporated – and he was angry enough to forget his manners. "Ballantine," Mr. Mikel snapped, "I hope my daughter isn't with you."

"As a matter of fact, sir, she is."

"Ballantine, I thought that nonsense was over. I specifically told you last year that I expected you not to see her in the future."

"Well, sir –"

"I'd hate to boot you out, Ballantine. In your small way you're a good man. But I'll not have you taking advantage of Deanna's inexperience and lack of discrimination."

"Sir –"

"Shut up, Ballantine. Put Deanna on the wire."

Chet turned, his lips tight, and went back to the kitchen. "Your father," he said. "Deanna, what's going on? He seems to have the idea that we're resuming where we left off."

"La, these old-fashioned fathers!" Deanna scurried to the living room but never answered the call. She pronged the handset firmly.

More happened while Chet stood as one dumb-founded, staring at her.

Someone rang the doorbell. Deanna scooted to the door and opened up wide. "Why, you old jealous cat." She laughed. "Chet, look at Indigo's face!"

Big Indigo stepped into the hall, hands hung loosely at his sides, his gray eyes narrowed and mean. "What cooks?" he asked Chet. "You know, Ballantine, for a bright fellow you can be rather stupid."

"I'd like to know what cooks, too," Chet said thoughtfully. "Did you tell the whole world where you'd be, Deanna?"

"Coming from you, Chet, that's very comical, very, very comical indeed. Indigo, I'm glad you came when you did. I've heard nothing but insults from the moment I arrived. He telephoned early this morning, Indigo, to ask me to intercede for Miss Abby Young. I told him her problems weren't my

77

problems. He began to rant, so I came over, thinking I could talk sense into him. But do you know what he said? He said my father is a bloodsucker! He said you're just a toad with ambition but no brains, trying to use me to get a job you don't deserve. He said –"

"Let's get out of here," Indigo told her. "I don't know what's wrong with you, Ballantine, but you've had it, believe me."

And still more happened while Chet stood there trying to grasp it all.

Again, the telephone rang. Deanna rushed to it and answered. At once, her voice lifted into stridency. "Daddy, am I ever glad you called! Chet hung up on you. He called you a dirty bloodsucker trying to wangle your way into high society by peddling me to the most blue-blooded bidder. Daddy, he *cursed* us! Daddy, if Indigo hadn't come when he did I –"

Deanna broke off with an impressive little groan.

She listened.

Very softly she said, "Yes, Daddy, I'll be right home. Next time I try to help anyone, I hope you'll spank some sense into me. Oh, it was horrible, just horrible."

Chet finally found his voice. "Please leave my house," he said.

Her lovely eyes faintly mocking, Deanna

78

went at once to the door. Indigo Norden just stood there, hands clenching and unclenching at his sides. "I'm trying to decide whether to punch some sense into you, Ballantine, or just boot you out of the corporation."

"In one minute, Norden, you may have some sense punched into you."

"Really?"

Chet took one step forward, then another, then another. Deanna called harshly, "Punch him, Indigo! Kick him!"

But it happened as Chet had guessed it would. Big Indigo Norden lost his air of toughness in a hurry. "I wouldn't dirty my hands on you," Indigo said, retreating. "I'll tell you this, Ballantine: I'd see a psychiatrist, if I were you."

Indigo left then, protectively holding Deanna's arm. The two cars zoomed away less than half a minute later. Chet thought he saw Deanna wave gaily at him as her roadster rounded the next corner, but he wasn't sure. He was sure, however, that her odd, unexpected visit had left him with some serious problems to grapple with.

Typically, Chet mentioned none of the events to Abby when he took her ice skating that afternoon at Municipal Pond. She apparently sensed he was troubled, because twice she asked if something was wrong.

79

"Just tired, I guess," he said each time. "I've been working on a tricky problem in flexible gearing. I can't go to formula to calculate the tensile stress produced by centrifugal force, because there are other stress factors involved. And then –"

"Please, no shop!" Sassy in her scarlet and black skating costume, her golden hair catching all the sunlight in the world, Abby darted away from him to execute a series of figure eights.

Still, Chet thought shop throughout the date, and he thought it during much of the night, and he thought it during his walk to work the following morning. By then it had occurred to him that Deanna Mikel and Indigo had conspired for some reason or another to ease him out of his job in the Development Lab. The whole thing, he knew now, had been staged for the specific purpose of arousing Mr. Mikel's paternal wrath. But why in the world did they feel it necessary to ease him out of the corporation? What would they gain?

But, again, the answers to vital questions eluded Chet, skillful thinker though he was. All he knew when he punched his time card was that for some reason or other this was the last time he'd punch a time card in the check-in room of the Development Lab.

Never a man knowingly to waste time, Chet went to his desk and began to look through it for personal belongings. The technical typist attached to his unit came in with coffee and looked askance when she noticed he'd not opened the safe-file. "Don't you feel like working today, sir?" she asked. "I wouldn't blame you. You've been battling that problem for weeks. I get tired of the same old problem myself."

"I think I'm out," he said dazedly. "I don't know the why of it, but I do know how it was accomplished."

The girl closed the door at once. "I can tell you the why of it," she said bitterly. "It's that Mr. Norden trying to swing his weight around. He's been talking against you for a couple of weeks."

"Why?"

"Because he has to make a show," the girl said. "So Mr. Dunlop thinks, at any rate. I don't understand this place any more. It was a lovely place to work until Mr. Norden started to skyrocket. Everybody got along just fine. But now the business people don't care about us, and we don't care about them."

An office girl knocked and entered. "Mr. Mikel wants you in his office right now, Mr. Ballantine," she reported.

Chet nodded woodenly and went upstairs.

He saw Norden in the doorway of the president's office, buttering Wente up. Chet went into the executive vice president's suite, filled his pipe while the secretary alerted the great man, then stepped into the handsome office and took the leather chair Mikel indicated.

Slim, graying, quietly good-looking and self-contained, Mr. Mikel indicated a paper on the blotter. "This is your letter of recommendation, Ballantine," he said tersely. "I never allow my personal feelings to intrude into purely business and professional matters. I'm certain you'll have no difficulty finding a suitable position elsewhere."

"You fire a man just because you're unable to control Deanna, sir, is that it?"

"Keep her out of this, Ballantine, or I'll tear up this recommendation."

Chet, beginning to become very angry, shook his head. "You can't buy me off, sir, with a letter of recommendation. If your daughter wants to promote Norden, that's her affair. If you want to let her do it, that's your affair. But when I'm sandbagged by an amoral pipsqueak of a badly spoiled daughter, that's my affair."

"It's your word against the substantiated word of Indigo Norden, Ballantine. I don't understand your resentment of me or of this corporation. You've always been treated well. The kindest thing I can think is that you have leftist tendencies you'd be wise to subjugate before they ruin your professional career. But be that as it may. Here's a good recommendation and my earnest hope you'll come to your senses."

Chet tore the letter into small pieces. A grunt sounded behind him. Norden. "Look," Norden said placatingly. "This doesn't have to be personal, does it, Ballantine? Take the bad with the good, that's my motto."

"I'm breaking you, Norden. You've gone too far."

The big man began to breathe heavily.

Mr. Mikel said soothingly, "Now, now, gentlemen, let's remember we're rational human beings. I'm sorry you tore up that letter, Ballantine. It indicates to me that you're less realistic than any scientific man ought to be. I'm not entirely without strength here, you know."

Chet asked, curious: "I wonder how many of the top boys you'll keep in the various labs, Mikel?"

"What's that?"

Chet turned to Norden. "I've said it before and I'll say it now in front of Mikel, Norden. You're an opportunistic fellow riding on the shoulders of people with talent and scientific know-how. You create nothing, you produce nothing. You have a good mouth, and you'll do anything and everything to get ahead. But basically, you're the one guy they can do without, as you'll discover when Mr. Mikel's nitwit daughter dumps you as she's dumped so many."

Mr. Mikel was on his feet, livid. "Get out of here, Ballantine," he ordered. "I wash my hands of you."

Chet left, taking with him the satisfaction of having seen the triumphant Indigo Norden blanch.

Chapter Nine

For Abby Young, it was a dreary Christmas season. Despite the decoration put up in the boarding house, despite the parties given by her friends in the corporation, despite a long-distance telephone call from her folks in Oklahoma, and despite the traditional all-day party given at the Cantwell Hotel by the corporation, it was among the dreariest Christmas seasons she'd ever spent. When the last gift had been given and received, when the last crumb of fruitcake had been devoured, when the last carol had been sung, she was more than delighted to put Christmas out of her mind. In the new year coming up, she resolved, she'd waste little time or attention on Christmas.

The day after Christmas, she telephoned the office that she'd not be in. At ten o'clock she boarded a bus for the Plymouth District of the old city. There was fresh snow to contend with, so the pace of the bus was slow, and her own pace was even slower as she walked the last few blocks to Chet's house. It gave her an odd pang to see the Christmas tree standing bravely lighted on a table near the living room picture window. How like her own improvident father Chet could be. Regardless of how poor the Young family had been, there'd always been a lighted Christmas tree somewhere in the Young home. One year, she recalled, it had been a "tree" wrought of branches her father had scrounged from here and there after all the Christmas tree lots had been closed on Christmas Eve. For three hours her father had sat working in the kitchen, tying the branches together with scraps of saved cord and then winding twigs and skimpy ends in and out of the bindings to hide the cord. Why, why, why? Her father had answered sturdily: "How can you be a Christian and ignore Christmas?" A strange man, her father. Always time for anything except earning a decent living for his family!

Her knock brought a cheery Chet to the door in sports slacks, a white shirt, a dark tie, and a gaudy cable-knit sleeveless sweater. "My sister's contribution to the merry Christmas," he explained the sweater. "Hi. Don't tell me you've been discharged, too?"

"No. You have to say one thing for Indigo, I'm afraid. He's always kind to the women he's used to get ahead."

"Is it wise for you to be here? Things were hot and heavy for a time in Mikel's office."

"You'd be working at Better Ways, I think, if I'd done the wise thing back in October. It all started, you know, when I refused to write that memo for Indigo."

"Bah."

He gestured for Abby to come in.

Vigorously, Abby shook her head. "You've licked your wounds quite long enough," she told him. "I have a list of companies that can use an engineer. Today I have a project: finding a job for a nice fellow."

Chet's face softened into something akin to fatuousness. "Do you know," he said, "that's the first compliment you've ever paid me. I'm deeply moved."

Abby had to look away, exasperated with both him and herself. What was happening to her? A few months ago there had been no thoughts whatsoever about Chet Ballantine. She had accepted him then with the same calm indifference she had accepted the weather. But now there were thoughts . . . the oddest thoughts. . . .

"You can't sit around and do nothing," she said hoarsely, "until you've used up your unemployment benefits."

"Wait right there," he said with sudden crispness. "And you owe me an apology, as you'll soon see."

The wait was brief. When Chet came outdoors, he looked the model of a model young engineer about to sally forth to a day's work. He backed his Dodge Dart from the garage, then got out to help her get in. He drove to Cantwell Bay, swung left into 1st Avenue, then swung right into Bedloe Lane. At the end of the crooked little street stood a small one-story building with a very steeply pitched, shingled roof. There was one large show window. Across this had been lettered: CHET BALLANTINE & ASSOCIATES. In smaller letters under the firm name were the words: RESEARCH, DEVELOPMENT, CONSULTATION.

Abby's pulse began to race.

"It's a sensible solution to the problem of employment," Chet said soberly. "I tried a few places and discovered that Mikel can play it tough and rough. On the other hand, the firms know my work and want my services. This is the solution. Who knows what accounts I'm handling? You see?"

"Chet!"

"Confidentially, Abby, the place was opened with a subsidy given me by Hogarth Enterprises. Strange, isn't it, that the company I've been bucking for Better Ways all these years is now the company that puts me into business?"

"Chet, how wonderful!"

He took her into the little building, asking her to see not the squalor but the potential. The first thing Abby noticed was a stench she'd become all too familiar with during her years of slum living. She came close to panic. She hung on, however, and presently the tension and fear subsided. "You're looking at a woman," she said dryly, "so I do see the squalor, and not all your big talk about the potential will distract my attention. We'll need two brooms, two mops, boxes of detergent and scouring powder. If we clean the place up during the week, we'll be able to paint it this weekend. Use latex paint, and it will be pretty and dry by Monday morning."

She looked at the furniture and shook her head.

"I'll research furniture prices and values," she told him. "I should think that two thousand would equip you nicely. I'll lend you the money, and if you dare to say no, I'll slap your face."

"Whoa, whoa, whoa."

But, in the grip of deep emotion, Abby shook her head fiercely. "You're here because of me," she said, "and don't you ever forget it. You didn't have to analyze that report. You knew you were taking a chance. All right. Now it's my turn to help you, and I intend to."

"I'm not broke, you see. I have about thirty thousand saved."

"That's impossible! Don't fib to me! The way you throw money around –"

"Not guilty, Miss Prosecutor. I've always saved a certain chunk each week: some for the bank; some for stocks and bonds. Any time you care to see my portfolio of gilt-edged securities, just let me know."

"Just the same!"

"I'll carry the ball," Chet said grimly. "It's idiotic of people to think that an engineer can be pushed around because he's an egghead. I have some interesting surprises for Better Ways, Incorporated."

Abby wondered, startled, if she'd ever really known Mr. Chet Ballantine.

He did allow her to help, though. He drove her home so she could pick up some old clothes, and then he drove to a supermarket so she could pick up cleaning supplies. Finally, he drove back to his place to change into levis and a work shirt and pack some things for lunch. They got back to his business establishment in time to do a preliminary sweeping of the office and shop area before lunch, and then after lunch they went to work in earnest.

For Abby, it was an oddly satisfying experience. Suddenly she came alive with happiness, and in her happiness she teased and prattled until Chet finally threw up his hands and asked, "You're the mouse I used to know, aren't you, named Abigail Henrietta Young?"

"Did I ever tell you why I was named Henrietta?"

"No."

Cute in her raggle-taggle work clothes, Abby sat on the floor and looped her arms over her knees. "I had an aunt named Henrietta. Everyone thought she had a ton of money, and you know how practical parents try to be. So to please the old girl, I was named Henrietta. Only she didn't have any money, you see. When my father found out about that, he started calling me Clem. Clem for

Clementine, my other aunt, the aunt who did have a ton of money. But by then it was too late. Aunt Clementine said she'd always hated girls named Henrietta and always would."

"Really?"

Abby swung her hands behind her and leaned back, her blue eyes sparkling. "I had the weirdest family, Chet. I wouldn't exchange it for any family on earth, though. I never liked the poverty, don't misunderstand. But I had the kindest father and the sweetest mother and the zaniest uncles and aunts you've ever heard of."

"What about lunch?"

"Goop, we've eaten."

He hunkered down before her. "You know," he said gently, "when a man's with a sassy ragamuffin and they're not doing anything, he's likely to become emotional. I think you should have that news flash."

Abby jumped up, not at all interested in *that*. They worked steadily from then until dark, and accomplished much. The next day, feeling too many aches and pains, Abby telephoned she'd not work that evening but she would look into the matter of furniture and shop supplies. During a lull in the library, she went upstairs to the office of the corporation's purchasing agent, Mr. Tenney. A long, bony man who liked his little joke, he said weakly, "Help, help, help," the moment he saw her. Chuckling, Abby put a list onto his desk. "I'm doing research, Mr. Tenney," she explained. "I'd like to know how much all this would cost and where it could be bought."

"Oh?"

He skimmed through the list. "Depends upon your purchasing power," he said. "If you have the leverage this corporation has, you could get it all for about three thousand. If you're buying for yourself or Chet Ballantine, say, it would cost closer to four."

Abby sat down. "What about Chet, Mr. Tenney?"

"It's common knowledge, Miss Young, that he's going into business for himself. The technical establishment here is all atwitter."

"Oh, that's too bad."

"Another way to handle this purchase problem," he said slowly, "is to allow a friend to look into the matter of good but second-hand things. It often happens that a firm on a government cost-plus contract refurnishes to build up the cost and the net. These things usually are handled through discreet wholesalers. I happen to know such wholesalers."

"I'd not want you to become involved in a war, Mr. Tenney."

"I don't happen to care what you do or

don't want me to become involved in, Miss Young. I've known Chet a long time. I resent what was done to him. I won't come out into battle openly, for obvious reasons. But I do have the right to spend my evening time as I wish, and I wish to spend it this way. Does he have cash?"

"Yes. This is my contribution, though. I feel I got him into all this."

"Probably you did. I wish I understood what young, presumably sensible women see in Indigo Norden."

"He makes you feel gloriously alive, sir. He makes you feel that something important is happening in your life. Frankly, he's quite a fellow."

"Well," he said philosophically, "you have to expect a silly answer when you ask a silly question. Now get out of here and let me think."

Abby all but ran, not wanting to say or do anything that might create in Mr. Tenney's mind second thoughts on the subject of aiding Chet. Back in her own office, she telephoned him the news, and then she summoned Alice Hull in for a conference.

"I want information," she told Alice crisply. "Faction fights faction, presumably, and it's important we appear not to be other than strictly neutral. It's easier to be neutral if you know what's going on and what pitfalls to avoid."

"Linda's excellent at getting information. I attribute it to her look of sweet innocence."

"But she mustn't appear to be fishing!"

"I understand," Alice assured her. She crinkled her brow. "I'd say, by the way, that Mr. Norden is also fishing. That secretary of his pops in at the oddest times and just sits unnoticed in a corner, seemingly reading. I've had to warn Linda to walk warily."

"Fine. You know, Alice, I'm discovering something about myself every day. Not too long ago I'd never have gotten involved in a thing like this. Now I rather relish the excitement. I don't know if I can get Chet back here where he belongs, but I'm certainly going to try."

In that moment, with her blue eyes flashing and her golden head high, Abby Young looked as dangerous as she was beautiful, Alice Hull thought.

Chapter Ten

Over the weekend, while helping Chet paint the office and shop, Abby generated several other interesting and promising ideas. While they were eating, they fell to discussing future prospects as Chet saw them. Chet said that if one had to be perfectly realistic about his prospects, one would have to assume there'd be a loss in annual income for from two to four years. "When you say fourteen thousand a year rapidly," he lamented, "it doesn't sound like much. But when you think in terms of finding enough work to net that for the wallet, then it sounds like a fortune. I have the rent here, the cost of supplies and equipment. Advertising. Notices in all the papers, appearances at meetings of professional societies, entertainment of people who can throw business to me. It all adds up, Abby."

"I could do some of that, couldn't I?"

"Oh?"

"Well, why couldn't I write a résumé of the education and accomplishments of Mr. Chet Ballantine? I could get all the information from our files. You have a wonderful professional record. I've checked. We have only three employees in the whole place who have basic patents in their names."

"What would we do – mimeograph the résumé?"

"No, sir. We'll have the thing professionally printed. Chet, if you want to be successful you have to seem successful. I'll write the thing; you read if for accuracy; then I'll approach one of the firms that prints for the corporation. I swing them some business from time to time, and I'm sure they'll cooperate."

"I don't know, Abby. I'll have to avoid conducting a raid on the clientele of other firms."

"Idiot. We'll send the résumé to all the other engineering firms first, with a letter suggesting you might be the ideal person to throw excess business to. I'd guess you could pick up at least five thousand a year that way."

"Well . . ."

But that was when the second interesting and promising idea occurred to Abby. "Another thing, Chet. What about royalties on those basic inventions of yours that Better Ways uses in five products? That's income, too."

"Well, the agreement was that I had a

96

good job with a future and that anything I developed ought to be used by them for free."

Abby sat up very straight. "Wait a minute, Chet! Now you don't have a good job with a future. Now they really are riding on your shoulders to make money only for themselves. I'd suggest you see a lawyer and discuss the entire matter with him. I know this. I know that last year the corporation netted four million dollars on those products in which they've incorporated your patented ideas and gimmicks. Surely they could pay you at least ten thousand a year for the right to use those ideas and gimmicks."

"They'd contest the claim. How would I pay for the legal costs?"

And that was when the third interesting and promising idea occurred to Abby. She asked casually, "How long would the other engineers and scientists work for them, Chet, if it became known the corporation cheated those who develop good ideas?"

She drew a deep breath.

The thing suddenly scared her.

"Good heavens," she asked, hardly daring to speak, "do you think Mr. Mikel acted without the advice of the corporation lawyers?"

Clearly, the thing scared Chet Ballantine, too. He stood up and ordered hoarsely,

"Back to the paintbrush, Abby, before we do something foolish."

But Abby couldn't drop her second and third ideas. All through the weekend they badgered her mind. Her instincts told her that she'd hit upon something big, and she couldn't argue her instincts into quietude. It was logical! The Sunday of Deanna's visit, everything had happened fast. The whole disgusting frame-up had been sprung suddenly on Mr. Mikel, and so sharply, too, that Mr. Mikel had lost his temper. Well, a person who lost his temper was hardly likely to behave in a sensible and logical manner, was he? Suppose, just suppose, Mr. Mikel had seen red and had continued to see red until after the discharge?

Late Sunday, while she was soaking in a bathtub fragrant with carnation bath salts, Abby remembered something Colonel Delaney had said about diversionary tactics. And that was when her fourth and most promising idea occurred to her. She went to bed excited, and she went to work excited, and around mid-morning, still excited, she casually strolled over to the Promotion Department to deliver a technical report on pulleys and belting to Indigo's secretary Harriet. Harriet naturally seized upon the opportunity to improve the shining hour, so

98

to speak. "So sweet of you to bring it over," Harriet cooed. "I wish I could let Mr. Norden thank you personally, but let's be realistic, shall we?"

"Fine with me. This is a busy day. There's so much interest in the reports Chet Ballantine wrote. I'm always curious when such an interest develops, so I asked a few questions. The interest stems from the fact that Chet Ballantine had some basic patents which the corporation uses in five money-making products. The engineers and scientists, bless their greedy hearts, are trying to figure out how many hundreds of thousands of dollars the corporation must now pay for the use of those patents."

Harriet croaked: "What?"

"Well, I've given you the gossip you wanted; now give me some to take back to my office. Why does Indigo Norden think his promotion to a vice presidency won't tear this company in half?"

Harriet said, not without a croaking dignity, "I never gossip, Miss Young. Confidential secretaries never do."

Gleeful, Abby returned to her office. She pulled in a number of Chet Ballantine reports and routed them off to various engineering and scientific departments. She'd just gotten the last one delivered when she received a call to report to Mr. Mikel's office at once. Indigo was there, looking drawn, and the corporation's chief attorney was there, looking bemused. Abby nodded respectfully to all of them and then advanced sedately to Mr. Mikel's large, kidney-shaped desk.

"Oh, do sit down, do sit down," Mr. Mikel invited her affably. "We have a few questions to ask you, Miss Young, and it may take time. Care for coffee? You may smoke if you wish."

"I'm fine as I am, sir, thank you."

"Well, that's fine. Miss Young, I understand there's a considerable interest in Ballantine reports."

"Yes, sir. I doubt there's an engineering or scientific group that doesn't have at least one Ballantine report right now."

"And there's speculation, I understand, concerning the financial arrangements we've made or presumably will have to make for the use of certain Ballantine patents?"

"Yes, sir." At that point, Abby contrived a melodious contralto laugh. "I believe Mr. Ballantine is now practically a millionaire, sir. It's odd how these practical and studious geniuses get carried away by ideas like that."

Mr. Mikel turned to the chief attorney. "Well, Shipley," he said, "there we are. Now what?"

"An interesting case, Mr. Mikel."

Indigo snapped, "It can't be. We can show that Ballantine was an employee when he developed those different gadgets and gimmicks."

Mr. Shipley eyed him haughtily. "Are you an attorney, Mr. Norden?"

"No."

"I thought not. An attorney seldom makes flat, unequivocal statements on matters he's not researched with the utmost care. Now it is interesting, of course, that Mr. Ballantine was an employee of record during his period of patentable creativity. But I'd have to study the terms of his employment before I could venture an opinion on the matter."

"No contract," Mr. Mikel said at once. "I'm afraid we're in the hole there. You see, Mr. Shipley, the firm has always had a good relationship with its engineers and scientists. Why not? We at the top have always been aware the firm owes its prosperity to these people. I can show that in the engineering and various scientific professions, we're known as an excellent firm to work for. So we made the same arrangement with Ballantine we've made with others. A good job, a good future, good security, good fringe benefits. We were able to demonstrate to him as to others that in the long run he'd make more money as a well-paid employee than as the beneficiary of relatively modest royalty payments."

"I see."

"You have to understand," Mr. Mikel said, "that while we do use these basic ideas in the products I've listed, they're not integral to the products. The products might not be as good if the ideas hadn't been incorporated into them, but they'd work and still be a good buy at the price."

"But you do use the ideas, sir, and these products do lead the field in their price range?"

"I would say yes."

"Did the products lead the field in their price range before the Ballantine ideas were incorporated into them?"

"I'd have to check on that."

Abby said most respectfully, "I've checked on it, sir. They didn't lead the field until after the ideas had been incorporated into them. The question was raised by an engineer who figured out it would cost several million dollars per product to retool for manufacture without those basic ideas."

Mr. Shipley shot a keen glance at Indigo Norden. "I would guess," he told Indigo, "that this is a most interesting case."

"Well, we did exploit the new ideas in our copy," Indigo pointed out. "I think it can be shown that the copy and the advertising built the products into leading positions."

Mr. Shipley smiled relievedly. "Well, if you can show that, Mr. Norden, our legal problem is vastly simplified. When may I have the brief?"

"The what?"

"The conclusive legal argument. Don't fret about the terminology; just give me the facts in a reasonably logical order."

Indigo shot a glance at Abby.

Abby looked off at the painting on the wall behind Mr. Mikel.

Indigo astonished her. "Mr. Mikel," he said firmly, "now that I'm to be a vice president, I think I ought to have a larger staff. The broader scope of my duties necessitates that request."

"Certainly, certainly."

"I wonder if I may bid for Miss Young's services, sir. I think she's misplaced. I'd cheerfully pay her ten thousand a year to work as my administrative aide. She could perform research, do writing, analyze ideas. Indeed, she does all this satisfactorily now in the library, as you have occasion to know."

Mr. Mikel smiled at Abby. "I knew you'd be offered the post," he told her, "which is why I wanted you here to listen to Shipley. I'm entirely satisfied you deserve the promotion. That report you did for Cleary was brilliant. It was also effective, I might add. The judge to whom it was submitted agreed with our argument and conducted the trial without benefit of reporters. The thief was released on probation at our urging, and all's well there."

"What about the detective, sir?"

"Who?"

"The thief promised to kick his teeth down his throat."

"Well, much is said during a moment of anger, Miss Young. We all know that, don't we?"

"Sir, that was no ordinary thief. He was selective in his choice of papers to steal."

"It's under proper surveillance, Miss Young, I assure you. Now, then, I take it the promotion is satisfactory and that you'll do the brief, as Shipley calls it?"

Indigo stirred on his chair. Her attention attracted, Abby met his fine gray eyes. Briefly, very briefly, the mind and character of Indigo Norden were naked before her. Suddenly, just like that, she saw why he'd been able to climb so high so fast. He'd trapped her! One step ahead of her always, he'd dangled the bait at exactly the right time and had trapped her!

Unless –

Quickly, in a voice she didn't recognize, Abby managed to say, "I don't want the job, sir, thank you."

Before anyone could argue, she excused herself and left.

Chapter Eleven

Indigo waited until January fifteenth, the day his promotion was announced, to argue the job matter with Abby. He waited until almost closing time. Then, impressive in tweed suit and overcoat, he came to say that he'd buy her dinner and take her home. He spoke with such confidence and charm Abby couldn't refuse either the dinner or the ride. Once they'd gotten into his Cadillac, Indigo said with rare tact, "It was generous of you, Abby, not to make a scene upstairs. I've always admired your generosity."

"Thanks, Indigo."

"It's a misplaced generosity in the case of Chet, Abby. This talk about infringement of his patent rights is pretty despicable. Better Ways has always been fair on such matters as payments."

"Better ways discharged him, Indigo, to

please a redhead enamored of you. You never used to fib. I always respected your basic honesty, so don't spoil it now."

He drove slowly through the gray winter afternoon, his eyes on the road ahead. Once they'd shaken loose from the rush-hour traffic on the main streets of Cantwell, he relaxed visibly and said, not without pride, "Actually, Chet was discharged to please me, Abby, not Deanna. I want to remind you of something many women tend to overlook. If I use help along the way, I also use my brains. No single woman and not even a group of women has anything to do with running the department I head. I must deliver something worthwhile. Mr. Mikel isn't the easiest man to please. And you know how Cleary battles me every inch of the way. So don't underrate my ability, Abby, or my importance in Better Ways, Incorporated."

"Why did they have to please you?"

"Simple. To too many people here I'm the fellow who once flunkied for a buck. To too many people here I'm the fellow who rides on the shoulders of others. So it seemed necessary to me to make a big splash to demonstrate my power here. Chet was the ideal victim. He'd become involved with matters not his business, and he'd made gratuitous comments about my usefulness here. I let Mr. Mikel know I'd quit if Chet wasn't fired. He weighed the two of us on his scale and decided I was worth more per ounce than Chet."

Resenting the mere thought of that, and hotly, Abby said to sting him, "You're changing, Indigo. You used to be a graceful winner. Now I detect smugness in you."

He wasn't stung. "I suppose that happens," he said comfortably. "In the beginning you feel that your triumphs are little ones, and they are. Then a day comes when you receive notification of your boost to a vice presidency and twenty-five thousand a year. That's a big victory, and you do become smug."

"When do you marry Deanna?"

That didn't sting him, either. "I haven't decided," he said candidly, "if I will marry her. A wife should be selected with care. Let's be honest, Abby. Have you looked at most women of fifty or so?"

"Well?"

"Some day, clearly, Deanna will be fifty."

"Have you looked at men of sixty or so, Indigo? Men shrink and wrinkle disgustingly, it's always seemed to me."

"But men aren't married for beauty, you see. And why else would anyone marry Deanna? An intelligent man, that is?"

"I think it's a dreadful thing, Indigo, to think a thing like that, let alone say it. You *are* becoming cocky, aren't you?"

He chuckled, and they drove on, took the Goose Point Bridge, then followed the curving shoreline to Abby's favorite sea food restaurant on Hook Point. Business was slow and they had their choice of tables at the window overlooking the water. There were gulls to be seen, but nothing else save the restless water and iron gray sky. Indigo looked for a time in thoughtful silence, then rested his forearms on the table and asked, "Shall we stop fencing with one another, Abby? I don't have to fence with you. I don't have to be here with you now."

A great truth occurred to Abby, and she uttered it. "But you do have to be with me now, Indigo. You're in the mood for the company of a particular woman. What's her appeal? I wonder. Some men respond to figures, others to eyes, others to posture, others to smiles. Does my smile enchant you? Anyway, it doesn't matter what the allure is. On this particular day of triumph you crave the company of a particular woman. So here we are, because you have to have that company."

"Do you honestly believe that?"

Abby nodded, feeling quite confident now. "You know it's true, too, Indigo! Well! I think I'll have lobster and Danish beer. It isn't often a girl dines with a corporation vice president, after all!"

"I think you should accept the job I've offered, Abby. Now be sensible just a moment. You have an interesting ability to gather and collate facts and then create persuasive arguments from them. But I'm the one who perceived that, not anyone else. And it so happens that by a rare combination of circumstances, you can earn good money through employment of your interesting ability. Notice I said rare? The same ability mightn't be at all salable in another organization."

"Still, I'd have to betray Chet, wouldn't I?"

"What do you owe him?"

"Gratitude. He got involved because of me."

"Then give him gratitude, Abby, not your financial security. You see, it comes down to that. Ten thousand a year isn't to be refused for noble reasons that have nothing to do with finance. You've told me a great deal about yourself. You've come from the slums. Hard road. Why wouldn't I know? I've walked it myself. Now, with a real chance in your grasp, you're going to be sentimental? Ridiculous."

"Still, I won't betray Chet."

He compressed his lips into a thin line. He

might have spoken angry words, but their waiter came for the order. Indigo ordered clam chowder, lobster, and Danish beer for two. His generosity to her and to himself restored him to good humor. "Ah," he said, "it's good to have bucks to spend that way. I feel that I'm approaching the end of a long, bitter war, Abby. Strange, that."

It was queer. For a moment, his happiness was her happiness, his triumph her triumph. Then, remembering, she shrugged. "I wish it had been won a bit differently," she told him. "But no matter. I've said I won't betray Chet. Now I'll deal with you, Indigo."

He asked, amused, *"You'll* do *what?"*

"My, what smugness!"

"But you're hardly in a position to deal, Abby. You take it on my terms or you're out in the gutter, too. I assumed you knew that."

All of Abby went cold.

"Abby," he said in silken tones, "I'm afraid you've always misjudged me. I'm afraid you've confused many generosities to you and other women with a generous spirit. I have none. I have reasonable gratitude to those who help me, and I'll repay favors if I'm not inconvenienced unduly. But, Abby, I'd not be where I am if I were just an amiable softy!"

"Indigo, I hope you're just joking."

"I'm not."

"Because if you're not joking, Indigo, I'll have to do many things to protect myself."

"Listen good, Abby. I let you off the knife point once because of past favors at the office. I forgave you that report that caused me such embarrassment. That made us even. Now it's a new ball game. I owe you nothing. I have a need in my office for a girl of your ability, and I'll pay well. But if you're not with me, then you're against me, and you're out."

"I see."

"Now I'll do this for Ballantine," Indigo said expansively. "I'll work a connection I have to get him a good supervisory job with an outfit in New Jersey. He'll get more money, we'll have no more headaches, and life will be happier and more prosperous for all of us. How's that?"

Abby glanced around the restaurant. She supposed they couldn't have found a lovelier setting in which to terminate the relationship that had begun when they'd both been in flunky jobs. Beautiful room, beautiful view, the aroma of fine food in the air, creamy napery and genuine sterling silver, crystal sparkling, candles glowing richly.

"So there we are," she said sadly. "Do we eat the expensive meal, and do you drive me home?"

"Don't make a hasty decision, Abby."

"It isn't a hasty decision," Abby said calmly. "Such principles as I've acquired along the way do mean something to me. And I find, you see, that Chet grows on a girl and that you don't."

"Now you shouldn't have said that, Abby. No dinner, and you'll have to walk home."

Abby had to laugh. Next, she beckoned imperiously to an attendant and asked for a telephone. Indigo settled back, laughing, like a Nero waiting to be amused. But when she also asked the waiter to give her the Mikel telephone number, Indigo came to the alert fast. "What do you think that'll get you?" he asked.

"Dinner and a taxi home."

Their eyes locked.

He shrugged. "Oh, all right," he gave in. "I did ask you here, after all."

There was no more conversation. Abby ate in most leisurely fashion so as to enjoy luxury while she could. But the meal had to end sometime, and around seven o'clock they were back in the Cadillac and en route to the Washburn boarding house.

Just as Abby got out of the car, Indigo did clear his throat. Abby looked up and made a discovery.

It was all over!

There was absolutely nothing she wanted to hear him say!

She nodded coolly, and went to the house without a single backward glance.

In her room, coolly, she sat down to think about Mr. Indigo Norden and to figure out a method to protect her interests and Chet's.

An irony occurred to her.

She smiled.

Then, cheerfully, Abby went early to bed.

Chapter Twelve

Deanne Mikel listened to the foghorn hooting away on Hook Point. The quavering, deep-throated sounds had an eerie quality that sent delightful shivers running through her. She felt a preposterous urge to climb aboard her boat and go zooming off through the fog in search of ghosts. Or was the urge really so preposterous? Her beautiful blue eyes dancing, Deanna darted up to her bedroom and telephoned Indigo Norden at his apartment. She had to ring fourteen times – she counted the rings – before Indigo came on sleepily, saying, "What a lousy time to call a fellow."

The testiness left his voice, though, after Deanna had murmured, "Hi, lover, pucker for a kiss."

Indigo laughed softly. "Always a pleasure," he told her. "Why aren't you asleep, though?"

"Restless."

"The cure for restlessness, I read somewhere, is useful work."

"Daddy won't let me work, Indigo. He claims it's unfair for a girl in my position to take work someone else may need. The Mikels are always fair."

"I'm glad to get that little flash. I'd not want to marry an essentially unfair person."

More delightful shivers ran through Deanna, but these had nothing to do with thoughts of spooks in the night. "I could kiss you and kiss you and kiss you," Deanna babbled, "when you say sweet things like that."

"What about some sandwiches and beer and maybe an early sail?"

"Indigo, would you? I've had enough sleep, honest I have. I went down to the library, thinking I'd read myself drowsy. But all I could think about was that old foghorn hooting and hooting away."

"I'll meet you at the marina in half an hour."

Gleeful, Deanna pronged the handset.

Knowing it would be bitter cold on the water, she put on her thermal underwear and her ski pants and shirt. Over the shirt she put on her quilted, waterproof jacket. Two pairs of wool socks, her fleece-lined field shoes, a green stocking cap and gloves, and she was ready for high adventure at four in the morning. She hurried downstairs. But as she was heading for the back door, the kitchen door opened and her bathrobed father came out into the hall, looking puzzled. "You sneak thief," Deanna teased. "There's something basically wrong with a man who'll raid his own refrigerator at four in the morning."

He swatted the seat of her pants.

Affectionately, Deanna kissed his cheek. "Old sandpaper face," she scolded. "I'm glad I'm not a man. I'd hate to have a sandpaper face."

"Where do you think you're going?"

"Out to find ghosts. Indigo's coming with me. We'll get sandwiches and coffee somewhere and maybe brood around until the fog lifts. Indigo thinks I should find useful work. He says work is a cure for restlessness."

"You're quite fond of him, aren't you?"

"Possibly."

"I wonder, though, if the obvious hasn't at least occurred to you."

Deanna wagged a forefinger at him. "From

the beginning, good sir. I'm a Mikel, after all! But there's no novelty in what Indigo is doing. All men use women any way they can to get what they want out of life. My, we women have a shocking time of it."

"May I ask a favor, Deanna?"

Deanna stopped smiling. She said, feeling hurt, "You don't ever have to ask for a favor, Daddy. I don't think any girl could possibly have a nicer father than mine. I mean that! I may seem zany at times, but I'm not zany enough to overlook the things Mom and you do for me."

"Well, the favor I'd ask is that you slow Indigo down. The boy is clever and resourceful, but at his age he lacks a certain depth only experience can give a person. He wants Miss Young discharged. He sent me a paper yesterday in which he asserts that she's working hand in glove with Chet Ballantine to embarrass the company financially and professionally."

Deanna had to look away. At the time she'd stuck the knife into Chet's back, she'd felt quite proud of herself. Since then she'd had second thoughts. The biggest thing that bothered her was that she'd lied to her own father. She'd not done that before; it still seemed incredible to her that she'd done it that once.

"I'm sure Miss Young is aiding Chet Ballantine to the best of her ability," Mr. Mikel said. "I pride myself on my ability to judge character, and I long ago pegged Miss Young as an essentially warm and loyal person. But any friend has the right to help a friend in a time of need. I couldn't punish Miss Young for a simple act of friendship."

"I don't know, Daddy, that I can do very much with Indigo. He's furious with Miss Young. At my suggestion, he took her to dinner the other evening and attempted to square her away on a lot of things, including her duty to the corporation and herself. She spewed hate, I guess. Right after he drove her home, Indigo came to me and said she's not the sort of person who should be in Better Ways for a day longer. I never have seen Indigo so angry."

"Well, tell him to stop concerning himself with Miss Young. You might also tell him, quite informally, mind, that you think the corporation will settle Chet's claim in a month or so."

"Daddy!"

He shrugged. "I blew my cork, I'm afraid, after you and I talked that Sunday. I acted on impulse, which is always unwise. We certainly did have a firm, if unwritten, agreement with Ballantine on those basic patents of his. Either we must take him back, if he wishes to come back, or we must make a cash settlement."

"Daddy, I'm so sorry!"

"What are *you* sorry for?"

"Well, after all!"

"It's interesting," Mr. Mikel said. "I once deplored your interest in Chet because I thought he'd never get anywhere to speak of. Now, because I blew my cork, he'll probably end up a millionaire."

"*What?*"

"Interestingly, all five of the products involved are making a tidy profit for us. To halt their manufacture and accomplish the necessary retooling would cost us, we estimate, in excess of four million dollars. Our attorney Shipley informs me that if we *don't* effect a settlement and *don't* halt marketing and manufacturing, we jolly well could lose that four million to Chet Ballantine. It's a problem. I don't want the problem complicated further by reprisals against Miss Young. Apart from the fact that I like to be fair, I like to be practical."

Dumbfounded, Deanna could only nod. When she stepped outdoors, she discovered that her tingling sense of happiness was gone. The dark morning was now just another dark morning, even though Indigo was waiting somewhere in it for her to come. Deanna drove gloomily to the marina and stepped into the all-night restaurant, just inside the marina entrance. Indigo was there, big, handsome, vital, cocky, a magic smile playing on his lips, a devastating twinkle in his fine gray eyes. What had he to be so cocky about? Deanna wondered. His great big brain had placed her father in a most awkward position!

"It's the way you walk, I think," Indigo said caressingly, "that makes you stand out in a crowd. I love that little bounce in your step."

"Flattery will get you somewhere."

But he noticed her constraint, and he noticed the worry in her eyes.

"Big problem?" he asked. "You should never brood over a big problem until you've discussed it with me."

Deanna ordered coffee and scrambled eggs and a toasted roll. She sat lost in thought until the breakfasts had been served and the attendant had returned to his station behind the counter. When she was positive she could talk without being overheard by the attendant, she said frankly, "Well, there is a big problem. And Daddy's asked me to help him with it. It's about the corporation."

He was all attention at once, she noticed.

"First of all," Deanna said, "Daddy has told me to tell you informally to stop pushing for Miss Young's discharge. He thinks it wouldn't be fair to discharge her."

"Fair play has nothing to do with a thing like this. People are either for you or against you. If they're against you, boot them out before they can harm you."

"Also, Daddy has to be practical. Mr. Shipley, the lawyer, thinks that if the company doesn't settle with Chet Ballantine, it could lose as much as four million dollars."

The blood seemed to drain from Indigo's face.

"Daddy thinks it would be foolish to get Chet Ballantine angry, Indigo. And Chet would be angry if we fired Miss Young for having helped him."

"I still say it can be shown that the copy and the promotion built those products up to money-making status."

"Then show it, Indigo! Right now, Daddy's in an embarrassing position because of what we did."

"Oh, don't fret about that. Is that what you've been fretting about? My dear child, he had to go because I needed to make a big splash. If he hadn't gone one way, he'd have gone another way. Has Cleary said anything about any of this?"

"Daddy didn't say."

"Cleary's the wheel to watch. Cleary resents

my swift rise in the corporation. I think he's afraid I may make executive vice president before he does. He should be afraid. If I made exec, Cleary would be out the next day."

"Why?"

"As I've said, people are either for you or against you."

"But Daddy always says personalities and attitudes aren't nearly as important as capability. I'm sure Daddy disliked you when you first came. There's a lot about you that Daddy wouldn't like. Daddy prefers the quiet type who gets things done without fuss and who never creates problems."

"Really?"

Deanna Mikel made a decision. "I think we'd better tell Daddy the truth about what happened that Sunday, Indigo. Then Daddy will rehire Chet Ballantine, and the major problem will be ended."

He dropped his fork – actually. And he wasn't so cocky just then, nor really as handsome as Deanna had always thought him. His face was a bit too fat; there was a definite indication of a double chin. And those fine gray eyes – weren't they just a bit cold?

"I think so," Deanna said. "I love my father very much, and I'd not want him to be embarrassed. If they have to pay such a sum of money to Chet Ballantine

– well, Daddy may not be made president after all."

"Whoa, Deanna. Do you know what would happen to me? I'd be outside looking in."

"Well, that wouldn't matter much, would it? I have oodles of money, and you'd be a luxury I could afford."

A slick of perspiration appeared on his forehead. "Listen," he said urgently, "you must either trust me and believe in me or it's no go. I know what I'm doing. I'm a vice president now because I have a brain. I'll forego the pleasure of firing Abby Young, if you insist, but only if you promise to trust me and believe in me."

Indigo smiled fully, reaching for her hand. Deanna sighed. "I could kiss you and kiss you when you're so clever and masterful," Deanna said. She did kiss his hand.

Chapter Thirteen

On February eighth, Abby was agreeably interrupted in the abstraction of a report on the application of a vibrating-link motion to a Better Ways shaping machine designed for operation on metal. She smiled gratefully at

122

Indigo's secretary. "Harriet," she announced, "you just couldn't have come at a better time."

Harriet looked at the diagram Abby had been studying. "Can you make sense out of things like that?"

"Yes and no. This figure is the plot of the motion of the working stroke of the mechanism that does the cutting. I'd guess the machine will sell quite well. Somewhere in the report the author shows there's a need for a machine of this capacity."

"I don't get it," Harriet said frankly. "I thought librarians were really just glorified file clerks."

"There's a bit more to the work than that. Some day you must sit at this desk with me and listen to the various service requests we get. Pulling a book in from the stacks is the least of our responsibility."

Harriet sat down. She was so ill at ease she was pathetic. Knowing that at best the girl was an emissary, Abby couldn't help but wonder what Indigo was up to now. It was an odd experience never to know from one day to the next just how and when she'd be booted out into the ranks of the unemployed. But it was even odder to sit completely unafraid of the raised boot. She owed Chet a large debt for teaching her security wasn't all it was reputed to be, all she'd always believed it to be!

"Mr. Norden thought you wouldn't mind looking at this memo," Harriet said huskily. "The memo concerns you."

"Really?"

"You know, Miss Young, sometimes people become angry for one reason or another and say much more than they should say. They say many things they don't mean. They say many things they really don't even think."

"I've heard that," Abby said wryly. "Naturally, I'm never guilty of such foolishness."

Harriet didn't smile. She sat with folded hands and a glassy stare until, to spare her further embarrassment, Abby did the kind thing and plucked the memo from the envelope. The words amazed her. "Has Indigo taken to drink?" she asked.

"It just so happens," Harriet said hotly, "that Mr. Norden is one of the finest men I've ever known. A lot of people here take pot shots at him only because they're jealous. It so happens that he's extremely kind and generous and fair. Something happened not long ago to make him think he'd been unfair to you. So he's written this memo to Mr. Mikel. How many vice presidents around here

124

would do a thing like that to make life easier for an ordinary worker?"

"It's a generous memo, Harriet. Am I supposed to thank him, or what?"

"Mr. Norden would like everything to be as it used to be."

"Everything?"

Harriet blushed. "Well, not really everything. Look. You and I know what the score is there, Miss Young. I don't like you any better than you like me, and for the same reason. And I don't like his infatuation with Miss Mikel any better than you like it, and for the same reason. But that has nothing to do with this. This is a purely business matter. Mr. Norden would like to feel you're no longer angry with him and that the department and the library can get along as well as it used to."

"Fine with me, Harriet."

Harriet got up to leave. "Thanks, Miss Young. If it's all right with you, I'll take this memo upstairs now."

Abby let her go, not eager to be reminded by Harriet's manner of the fool she herself had played for far too long. But it was impossible for her to return to the abstraction of the technical report. There was, she felt certain, a significance in the memo that she'd failed to grasp. You could always be sure there was method in any seemingly mad act done by Indigo Norden. His climb hadn't been accidental or willy-nilly. Step by step he'd risen in conformance to a plan. At this late date Indigo wasn't abandoning his plan merely to mollify her. Something was up! But what?

She was still wrestling with the question when Mr. Cleary stepped into her office at eleven-thirty. Mr. Cleary smilingly laid Indigo's memo on her desk. "Mr. Mikel thought you might wish to see this, Miss Young," he said. "I hope you'll notice my approving signature under Mr. Mikel's."

Abby went through the pretense of reading and of showing girlish surprise.

The vice president of designs nodded. "I thought you were an accomplished actress, young lady," he told her. "Now I know you to be one. Norden's secretary told me she'd shown you the memo."

Abby shrugged, unabashed.

Mr. Cleary sat down. His icy eyes appraised her attractive, good-humored face, and his brow furrowed. "I find you interesting," he announced. "You have a youthful softness and prettiness, but you have a youthful savagery, as well, which you conceal better than most young women do."

"Sir, I insist a woman isn't savage."

"Nonsense. I looked over that report Ballantine sent the company in justification

126

of the five million he's asking for his patents. Ballantine never wrote that report. You did. And here and there in the report were sharp little digs only a savage would make. Does Ballantine seriously believe he'll get the five million?"

"No, sir."

"What does he expect to get?"

"His job, a raise in salary, a guaranteed royalty on his patents for a forty-year period."

"He couldn't very well be given his job, you know. I tried to intercede at the time, Miss Young. I've always loved Ballantine's work. He thinks of everything. His designs are clean from conception through execution. But this is a personal matter to Mikel, and he won't go that far."

"Mr. Ballantine realizes that, sir. Probably the thing will go to court. Much will come out during the trial, you may be assured of that. I imagine you'll lose talent as well as money. I've looked over some of the material Mr. Ballantine has, and I agree with him that it's dynamite."

"Dynamite?"

"Sir, I didn't finish telling you the rest of Mr. Ballantine's terms. Mr. Norden would have to be discharged."

"Oh."

Abby shrugged. "Sir, I'm sure you know of

my former infatuation with Mr. Norden. I'm not the first, and I won't be the last. There's no rhyme or reason to it. I could tell you many horrible things about Mr. Norden that you've never even guessed. But he looks at a woman in that delightful boy-man way, and somehow he gets a stranglehold on her emotions. The odd thing is that right now, right this very minute, I feel sorry for him, as a woman feels sorry for a naughty little boy she's enormously fond of. I'd do anything not to break his heart, anything at all. But Mr. Ballantine won't yield on that point. I've begged and I've pleaded. The answer remains no."

"It isn't like Ballantine to be vindictive."

"That may be, sir, but those are his terms."

"Too bad."

Mr. Cleary stood up and started toward the door. He stopped and returned to the chair. "I wonder," he asked, "if you'd like to work for me, Miss Young. I'm a hard man. I expect work for pay, and I don't fiddle-faddle with such nonsense as fathering or mothering an employee along. I can give you a future here, however, if you want one."

"Yes, sir."

He nodded. "I like people who can make swift decisions. Very well. We'll swing you up to my office on the first of March. We'll start you out at nine thousand a year. Norden gave me an excellent idea when he bid for your services as administrative aide. You have a fine background knowledge of the work we do here. You think, and you write. You'll spare me for more important duties."

"Thank you, sir."

"No thanks necessary, Miss Young. Now, then, let's go to Norden's office, shall we? I'm charged, it would seem, with disposing of the Ballantine matter once and for all."

Abby inhaled deeply. "May I fix my face, sir?" she asked. "I have my pride."

"Certainly. Ballantine is worth a thousand of him, though, you know."

"My mind may know it, sir, but there are emotions, too, I'm sorry to report."

He snorted, and then he gestured for her to go fix her face.

They reached Indigo's office in the executive suite just a few minutes before lunch. Indigo, Abby discovered, had done things up big. The office was paneled beautifully in walnut. The furniture was Danish modern. Royal blue carpeting ran from wall to wall. Carpenters had transformed the wall with three windows into a window-wall that afforded a breathtaking view of the city and bay. And, would you believe it, Indigo had equipped the office with a stereo record player from which, soothingly, came the muted music of a Brahms!

Indigo was in his hearty executive mood. "Cleary," he said, pumping hands, "I want you to pop in often. I know you have the edge in experience and know-how, and I want to learn all I can from you."

"I'm to settle the Ballantine matter," Mr. Cleary said without preamble. "You once mentioned you could show that the success of the products involved is attributable to copy and promotion – to advertising in one form or other, that is. Were you just talking, Norden?"

"Sir, I didn't reach this office through talk."

"Of course you did! Oh, you've done good work in spots, but good work alone doesn't bring a man up here so rapidly. I asked a question. I'll rephrase it. What can you give us to support your statement?"

"History of the products before and after promotion was undertaken. History of the products even though others have come up with a variation of Ballantine's ideas. Then, about Ballantine: figures can be produced to show he drew wages from the corporation while he was working on those ideas. He drew supplies. He had office and shop space. Quite a lot of evidence, sir."

"I doubt any of it means much, Norden. Write it up, however."

"I'm trying to find a writer."

"Why? You're our promotion specialist. You must be familiar with the written word. I've seen hundreds of beautifully written papers which were credited to you."

But Indigo, in that moment, was truly magnificent. Laughing, eyes twinkling, he held a hand up authoritatively. "Now just a moment, Cleary," he said. "Up here, between two vice presidents, there oughtn't to be bunkum. You know and I know that Abby Young here did those papers. A busy man, Cleary, has no right to use his valuable time on papers the hired help can write."

Suddenly, in the icy eyes of Mr. Cleary, Abby saw a terrible gleam Indigo apparently did not see. Goose pimples formed on her back.

"Norden," Mr. Cleary said, "I never knew Miss Young did your papers. Oh, I knew she aided you with them here and there, but I didn't know she actually had planned them and written them. I'm sure others up here don't know it, either. I heard several of our colleagues say just this morning that it was grand to have a clear thinker and good writer up here."

"Oh, I planned them and outlined them, of course."

Abby had to look at Indigo then.

Cockily, he gave her the old smile, the old caress with his eyes. "Tell the man," he said, "will you?"

"Norden," Mr. Cleary ordered, "write me that paper today, please. A matter of millions is involved. I assure you that if we must settle for millions, you're out on the street."

"I, sir? But Mikel fired him!"

"You requested it, Norden. Ironically enough, you requested it in writing."

The irony hurt. Indigo Norden grunted with the pain of the hurt.

Chapter Fourteen

Her heart drumming, Abby Young generously gave herself the afternoon off. Alice Hull said enviously, "It must be grand to be a wheel." Alice stopped looking so envious when Abby informed her that as of March first the library would be headed by one Alice Hull. "Take a year off," Alice urged. "Boss lady, I could kiss you!"

Abby also generously treated herself to a

ride to Chet's place in Bedloe Lane. She found Chet out back in the shop, contentedly at work on the machine lathe. He said, "Watch out for grease." He continued work for ten minutes, intent upon the job. When he turned the lathe off, he gave her some news. "This is a custom-designed valve for a high-pressure hydraulic system," he explained. "I got the order through one of your sales letters. When you can get around to it, will you go talk turkey to those people? They want me on a retainer basis."

"How'd you like to be a millionaire?"

"Well, I have news about that, too," Chet said. He turned off the lamp over the lathe and led her up front to his elegant office. "My lawyer thinks the best I can hope for is royalties from here on in. I couldn't lie on the witness stand, you know. So what's gone on before this doesn't count."

"Agreed. But you have a club. If you don't let them use your things, they'll have to stop manufacturing and retool. It would be cheaper for them to give you a million."

"Wrong again. The lawyer says all they have to do is establish what would be a reasonable royalty rate. A reasonable offer, plus the fact they've been fair in the past, would give them the victory."

"Who defines the word reasonable?"

"The fact that I accepted what I did all along, without complaint, mind, would be considered when the judge defined the word."

"Oh, dear."

"Will you mind marriage to an ordinary working man?"

"Now you're going much too fast, Chet. I didn't know I was involved in all this for love and kisses and cook my breakfast, darling."

He said chidingly, "Be a big girl, Abby. What else are you in this for? You could've sold out to Indigo any time if I were just another fellow to you."

"Well, I got you into this mess because once, back in October, I refused to write a certain memo."

"So, guiltily, you turn your back on Indigo and ten a year to help me?"

Along about then, Abby's cheeks began to burn. "Well," she said stiffly, "I suppose friendship doesn't mean as much to you as it does to me. Let me tell you something about Abby Young. Colonel Ned Delaney was dead wrong one day when he accused me of being a loner. I'm far from that. You'd be surprised if you knew how many letters I still write to people I knew in the slums. But I don't like people easily. And it's much more difficult for me to become fond of people. And it's even more difficult for me to become friends with people. But when I do make a friend, that friend becomes a part of me. And when that happens, Chet, I don't find it at all difficult to turn my back on a tiger like Indigo or to refuse a ten-thousand offer that'll be withdrawn the moment my usefulness in a certain situation is ended."

"Still . . ."

"I came running to beat Indigo here, Chet. Shall we talk about that?"

He sat behind the desk, really quite handsome in his black and red wool shirt. "Why would Indigo come here?" he challenged.

"Because, Chet, I think Indigo's had it. I know that sounds cockeyed, his recent promotion considered. But I saw a man, Mr. Cleary, do a terrible thing this morning. He cold-bloodedly and cruelly forced Indigo to expose a weakness, and then he exploited that weakness by ordering Indigo to do something Indigo had just admitted he couldn't do. And he put it all on an or-else basis."

"Well, things are looking up!"

"Did you know, Chet, that success is a relative thing? It all depends upon what's important to you. Now take Indigo and his vice presidency. He's cut a lot of corners to reach that posh office. Now he's there. But he's in a trap, too. Now, for the first time

135

in his life, poor Indigo has something worth defending. But is this competent opportunist, this successful man, capable of defending the thing he's won? Can he enjoy the success? And if he can't, then where's the success, where's the prize he did so much to win?"

"I couldn't care less about Indigo. I have some other news for you, Abby. I mentioned that one of the corporation's competitors, Hogarth Enterprises, gave me a subsidy so I could open this place. Well, they've been thinking things over since you sent them a copy of that brochure detailing my background and accomplishments. The fact I had so many basic patents interested them. They'd like me to take over direction of a small unit doing very advanced research and development. Cloud Nine stuff, all in all."

"Chet!"

"I'm not the administrative type, you know. They offer twenty thousand a year. We'd work here, and they'd reimburse me for all my personal costs and take over the place. Changes would be made, sure. Bars on all the windows, a permanent security guard. As I've told you, it's Cloud Nine stuff."

"How can you refuse?"

"The trouble with administration, it's always seemed to me, is that it leaves you so little time for working on projects that are important to you. I'm an M.E. first, last and always. I love machines. Machines accomplish useful work, work that has to be done if an exploding world population is to have all the goods it needs. I know a lot of people hate the machine because they think the machine deprives people of jobs. But put it this way. If it weren't for the machines that really produce them, few could afford cars or radios or stoves or refrigerators. So there'd be grave unemployment, rather than the pockets of employment that exist today."

"You don't have to sell me, Chet."

"I'd like to refuse the job. To be honest, I'd like to be back at the old stand in Better Ways, Incorporated, right now."

"I'd guess they'd take you back."

"Norden would have to go. After that filthy trick he pulled on me that Sunday, Norden has to go. I couldn't work in a place where he was vice president."

"I think —"

But that was when a Cadillac halted before the little building and big, confident, smiling Indigo Norden got out to survey the scene with scorn. Three powerful, forceful strides brought Indigo inside. "Well, well, well," he said to Abby, "it's strange how predictable you are; very strange."

Chet came to his feet. "I hope you'll stand

your ground this time, Norden," he said. "I want a fair swing at your jaw."

"Any time, Ballantine."

Grinning joyfully, Chet zipped around the desk. "Like now, Norden?"

Two-hundred pounder though he was, Indigo recoiled two or three short steps. "Are you crazy?" he rumbled. "Why make this a personal issue? Business is business."

"Including that monkey business at my home, Norden?"

"Look, anyone crazy enough to let Deanna into his home deserves to have things like that happen to him. But we could discuss that all day and get nowhere. I came to show you why I'm a vice president, Ballantine, and why you don't come back to Better Ways except on my terms. What you happened to overlook, you and Abby there, is that money talks in this world, talks even to lawyers. I've bought yours. I know every weakness of your argument, and if you think old Indigo's going to be made the fall guy now, you have another think coming."

"Oh, you'll fall," Chet said. "I guarantee it."

"We'll take you back, give you a few bucks to cover the royalties due you since you were canned, and that's it."

"No dice."

Indigo got the door open. "Well, you heard the offer, fellow. And if I were you, Abby, I wouldn't bother going back to work. I'm in the saddle again, and this time Cleary had better realise that."

Abby just managed to catch hold of Chet as Chet bulled toward Indigo. By the time Chet had pulled free, Indigo was back in the Cadillac and driving away.

Chet was furious. "Did you have to grab me? Did you? That fellow's all mouth!"

"And brains."

"Brains?"

Trembling with reaction, Chet sat down. Abby fetched him water and made him drink every cold drop. "I used to have to do that as a child," she told him. "It was Mom's way of making me cool off. Now listen, Chet. The last thing in the world to do just now is to become involved in a fistfight with Indigo. I don't say he wanted to be punched just now, but if you had punched him and left a bruise, he'd have exploited that this afternoon up in the executive suite. Now get on the telephone, please, and ask for Mr. Wente. Tell him you won't settle your case for less than three million dollars. Tell him that unless you're given a decision this afternoon, you'll start a lawsuit tomorrow."

"But I've told you –"

"Chet, you can't convince me that Better Ways has become a great corporation by using tactics such as Indigo's. You can't tell me that they don't look beyond today over there. You have three things in your favor. You have the patents, and you weren't discharged for incompetency. You haven't been paid your royalties, and they did break their unwritten agreement with you. Finally, you have the respect of the technical and scientific people there, and you have the respect of others in this community. I don't think your case is quite as weak as your erstwhile lawyer and Indigo would have you believe. May I ask you one question?"

"I wanted to pop him right on the button. I did!"

Laughing, feeling most maternal, Abby distracted him from frustration in the only way she could think of: she caught hold of his ears and kissed him full on the lips and then crooned, "My heap big warrior!" The kiss did distract him, all right!

"The question I want to ask, Chet, is when your lawyer gave you all the bad news you told me?"

"About ten minutes before you came."

"I see. And along came Indigo not too much later to gloat. I'm sure he did buy your lawyer, but I'm not sure your case is as poor as that lawyer and Indigo claim."

"Do that again," Chet demanded.

"What?"

"Kiss me that way again."

"Will you telephone Mr. Wente?"

"After I've been kissed that way again."

"But if we *did* marry, Chet, we couldn't live on kisses!"

"Have I asked you to marry me?"

Lord, Abby thought, throwing away the last of the pretenses to herself, this fellow would be fun. He might drive her crazy, but he'd be fun.

She sat down and waited for Chet to do as he'd been asked.

Chet just waited, chin high.

Abby tried batting her eyelashes at him.

"Cute," he said. Still, the trick didn't work.

But there was always a way, Abby remembered, if a woman just got in there and pitched.

"To please me?" she asked in a wheedling tone.

Chet sighed, and reached for the telephone.

Chapter Fifteen

On Saturday morning, quite reluctantly, Abby finally resorted to the tactics she'd worked out after her unpleasant sea food dinner and argument with Indigo Norden. She taxied to the marina, located the Deanna Mikel boat, and sat down to bask in the surprisingly warm late-February sunshine. An old gaffer came along to bum coffee money from her. Cheerfully, she gave him a dollar. "Hey," he said, "hey!"

"Mister," she told him, "I've been so poor in my time you wouldn't believe it."

"I'll get you coffee, okay?"

"If you wish."

He did wish. He brought coffee for her and coffee and pastry for himself. He sat on the bench and ate and drank noisily. "I can't work," he explained. "Even if I was young enough, I'm too lazy."

"That happens."

"It's sure funny how God makes people, girl. I don't mean me, understand. Old Nick made me. But take you and take the redhead that owns yonder boat. I don't have to price your duds in town to know you're a working stiff. But that redhead, you could starve dead in front of her, and all she'd do would be laugh."

"Oh, I don't know."

"She a friend of yours?"

"No."

"It's okay, though, about her. This guy she's got, he's playing her for a real patsy. Things sure even up in the end, I guess."

"Big, handsome fellow with black hair and lovely gray eyes?"

"Well, he's big, all right, but I don't know about handsome. To me, he looks like a hard-boiled shark that knows how to handle women."

Abby laughed weakly.

"Hey," he said, "what are you laughing at?"

"Well, I was just thinking. I once knew a writer who told me there are as many worlds as people and one world more – the real world made by God and perceived imperfectly by man. And then this writer said it's the same with people as with worlds. He said that one person is really ten thousand or ten million persons – a different person to each set of eyes that looks at him. For instance, I never saw a shark in Mr. Norden."

The old gaffer laughed, with a foolish looseness that betrayed his senility. "What

God done," he said, "was to make girl children with eyes that don't see men like men see men."

A car came along and nosed into a parking slot just beyond the marina entrance. The old man crossed himself and scuttled away as if afraid of the evil eye. Presently Deanna Mikel came to the slip to look over her beached boat. Deanna was fetching in a green corduroy slack suit piped with scarlet. Her carriage was saucy, her self-confidence and joy in living almost sublime. Abby hated to mar the girl's day, but it did seem to her that even the beautiful Deanna ought to learn something about Newton's law of compensation. Easily, thoughtfully, Abby walked over and ranged herself beside Deanna. She gazed down at the boat, too. "I've seen better," she announced. "I've seen better men than Indigo Norden, too."

Deanna looked up, straightened up. "Well, well, well," she said, "if it isn't the ex-librarian."

"Not ex, Deanna. Mr. Wente hasn't yet turned the corporation over to Indigo."

"Definitely, ex. I personally guarantee it."

"We'll see. I wonder, Deanna, what you'll wear in court? Indigo prefers quiet tweeds, but you don't seem the quiet-tweed type."

"Why would I ever appear in court?"

"You mean Indigo hasn't told you?"

"Miss Young, if you expect these tactics to accomplish anything, you'll be disappointed."

"I'm not entirely sure. We have a clever little strategy worked out. Chet Ballantine was discharged by the corporation. When he was discharged, the corporation broke its unwritten contract with him. Now how can the corporation justify the discharge? And it must justify the discharge, you see, or give the presiding judge good reason to think it was trying to avoid paying Chet for the patent devices it was using."

"He was incompetent!"

"My dear girl, we have the official commendations the corporation gave Chet. We have the proof that many organizations in this city think highly of his work. I'm sure they can't plead incompetence."

"And I'm sure –"

"So we get around to you, my dear Deanna. We put you on the witness stand and put you under oath. We then ask why you invited yourself to Chet's house one day. We ask many, many questions. Are you sure you won't make a slip under all that questioning? Are you sure Indigo won't say something to leave you holding the bag?"

"I don't scare, Miss Young. Anything else?"

"A number of interesting surprises, Deanna."

Deanna looked back at the boat. "I do wonder," she said, "why you ex-girl friends of Indigo can't take your lickings gracefully."

"Oh, we do. For instance, Deanna, he's entirely yours. No competition. But getting back to the testimony you'll have to give: Chet never did get a chance to tell his side of the story to your father. I wonder what your father will think when he hears the story."

"My word against Chet's!"

"That's the whole point, Deanna. Your word against Chet's. Now we spring a delightful surprise. Will he or won't he marry you, this Indigo Norden? If he says yes, or if he does, then obviously your testimony against Chet will be deemed biased. Testimony to buy a man's hand in marriage, you see. Clever?"

"Why, you little –"

"And why would Indigo marry you, Deanna? If the case is won by the corporation, he's home free. The grateful corporation couldn't boot him out even if you and your father wished it. In fact, Indigo would look very, very good for having gotten Better Ways out of a jam your father put the corporation into. I'd say that Indigo has everything to gain and nothing to lose by refusing to marry you."

"I'll scratch your eyes out!"

"No, Deanna. Where I was born and raised, I learned early to take care of myself. Now, then, do you want to prove that everything I've said about Indigo is or isn't true? Chet won't settle now. It was the last straw when Indigo came to try his bluff and to fire me. You definitely will be called. There isn't anything on earth you can do to keep from testifying, believe me. So go ask Indigo to marry you. You got him into the job with your act that Sunday. Demand your reward. Or do you lack the nerve?"

Deanna walked away. She said nothing, but words were unnecessary.

Amused, Abby taxied back to the boarding house. She telephoned Indigo and told him it might be worth-while for him to take her somewhere for lunch. Being Indigo, the veteran of hundreds of such campaigns, he laughed softly and told her to put on something yellow. Abby did, and in the Cadillac, Indigo said with reasonable sincerity, "I always love you in yellow. I'm sorry about the way things worked out. I know you won't believe that, but it's true. I'm always sorry when I reach the kiss-off with a beautiful woman. A part of man's life goes away with each woman."

"But there are always more, Indigo."

"How do you like that! How about that, eh?"

Abby settled back in the seat. She wondered, being human, if this were the last time she'd ever ride in a Cadillac. Chet would always earn a good living, she was positive, but there would inevitably be those five children she'd always wanted, a proper home for those children to grow up in, and –

"We'll talk before lunch," Indigo said. "I suspect neither of us will want to be overheard. I'm sorry it all came to this, Abby. There was a time, really, when I thought that if I married anyone, it would be you."

"Not Deanna, then?"

"Frankly, no. Mikel hasn't acquitted himself too well in this Ballantine matter. I overheard Wente telling him so. It's likely that Wente will now push that push-button board of directors of his into giving him another two or three years at the helm. True, corporation bylaws require presidential retirement at sixty-five, but you have a board of directors so you can change the bylaws when you wish to. Well, in three years Mikel will be sixty. At the same time, I'll have had an opportunity to develop my position, create alliances. Three years from now I'll probably be able to make out a strong case for turning the presidency over to a younger man, a man

148

possessed of the drive and ambition needed to make this corporation one of the greatest in the nation."

Abby's mind reeled. "Indigo," she said, "I'll say this for you; you know how to spin dreams."

"I always could," he said matter-of-factly. "And I'll tell you why they always come true for me, Abby. Not only do I have the courage to dream big, but I have the courage to believe in my dreams, to fight, to plan, to conspire to make them come true. There's what's wrong with most people today. They're takers, not creators; they're conformists, not doers. I have much more respect, really, for the radicals of the Thirties than for these bright people of today who have everything but the courage to use the educations they've been given. The radicals believed in their dreams. The forty-hour week! I read somewhere that when that was proposed in the early Thirties, it was denounced as a wild-eyed fantasy that would reduce this country to the status of a fourth-rate power. But the radicals believed in their dream, fought for it, lived to see it come true, and lived also to see this country become the most powerful on earth. But the conformist of today, the puling pipsqueak who finds a Communist under every bed ... he won't even risk changing jobs for

149

fear he'll lose his pension rights. At twenty-five or thirty, yet, he's actually more worried about his old age than –"

"Cut, Indigo."

"Cut?"

"A very clever gimmick, Indigo. You talk wildly, and I'm supposed to reply in kind. But since you own the tape-recording, you can erase your wild chatter but preserve mine."

"Who has a tape-recorder in the car?"

"You have."

He exhaled his breath gustily. "Sometimes you frighten me, Abby," he said. "You're almost clever."

"Well, as we've mentioned more than once during our odd association, we both come from the slums; we've both had to use our brains to get ahead. I've had a talk with Deanna, Indigo. I've told her we are pressing the lawsuit to an ultimate conclusion. She'll be called as a witness, and so will you."

"What ever for?"

"The reason for the discharge of Chet Ballantine will have to be brought out. The corporation, of which you're vice president, can't have it two ways, Indigo. If Chet was incompetent and deserved to be fired, why did the various officers write all those commendations, and why does the corporation use his inventions and ideas? But if he was fired by

150

Mr. Mikel for personal reasons, then how does the corporation prove it wasn't trying to get out from under paying him for the use of his inventions and ideas?"

"My dear girl –"

"I told Deanna you'd not marry her, Indigo."

He sucked air.

"I thought you'd appreciate the irony," Abby said gently. "The man who's climbed so high over the shoulders of silly, helpful women must now lose to a woman. If you marry Deanna, she wins. If you don't marry Deanna, I win. Cute?"

The car swung wildly toward a curb. Indigo braked it savagely and curled his fingers into a fist. "I ought to punch you slap-happy," he snarled.

"But you won't. You know that nothing on earth would keep Chet from finding you. You're afraid of Chet, Indigo, aren't you? In fact, you're afraid of men, period. That's why you've always concentrated on women. Women are pretty, women are emotional, and best of all, they can't punch you when they find out."

"Get out of my car."

"But you forgot one thing, Indigo. You forgot that the brains that could help you upward could also help you downward. My, what an interesting section of town!"

And, cheerfully, Abby got out of the Cadillac to figure out a way to get back home.

Chapter Sixteen

The ringing doorbell roused Chet Ballantine from a reverie. He went mechanically to answer, but halfway to the door he remembered another Sunday morning he'd opened that door to grief. Chet went out the back door and walked warily around the side of his house. He was very pleased with himself. "I'm as good as any kid you can think of," he bragged. "Even I learn the danger of playing with matches, Deanna."

The redhead whirled, then grimaced. "Oh, be a big boy," she snapped. "I wish to talk to you."

"Talk."

"Not here. Now be sweet and let me in."

"Honey, if you set so much as a foot in this house, I'll telephone the police. Better still, you get on the other side of that fence."

"Chet, will you listen?"

"Nope. Not until you're on the other side of that fence."

She was so angry she all but punched holes into the brick path with her heels as she went back through the gate to the sidewalk. Chet closed the gate and then backed off five or six feet. "I'm getting away from you," he explained, "so that neither you nor your father can claim I took a swing at you. Now what did you want to talk about?"

"I want you to cancel that lawsuit. It's very embarrassing to Daddy."

"Now isn't that too, too bad."

"If you've lost a few nickels and dimes, I'll reimburse you. I'll give you my check here and now."

"A birdie tells me you don't have three million dollars in your checking account."

"Chet, you asked for exactly what you got. You were always mean to me. And you made all those mean remarks about Indigo."

"Some day, Deanna, I'm going to hit that big bag of wind and tricks right in the old breadbasket."

"Please, Chet, this is very important to me."

"Nope."

She went panicky. "What do you really want? Tell me what you really want? You can go back to the corporation. Miss Young can have her job back. And I'll give you ten thousand dollars."

"I want Norden's throat, Deanna, that's all."

"I love him!"

"I know. They all love Indigo Norden, don't ask me why. Abby's told me something an old gaffer told her on the marina the other day. Girls don't have eyes that see men as men see men. Something like that."

"There's nothing you can do, Chet, nothing at all, to get Indigo out of the company. And you can tell Miss Abby Young that he'll marry me any day I wish."

"I'll tell Abby that. Anything else before you leave?"

"Chet, please?"

A ghastly thing happened then, something Chet knew would give him the creeps whenever he thought about it in the years to come. Miss Deanna Mikel, the beautiful redhead whom so many had chased after to their regret, now put on her sweetest smile and opened her lovely eyes wide. Confident of her allure, she cooed, "You'll do this for me, please, won't you, Chet?"

But something else happened, too, something that spared him the necessity of giving her the shock of her life. A limousine came into the block and glided to a halt behind her parked car. A portly, white-haired man alighted and said amusedly, "Deanna, don't tell me the scoundrel is forcing you to *beg* for admittance."

Deanna squeaked, "Mr. Wente, what are you doing here? I mean, in spite of your age and all."

He said, "Hmmm." He said, "Now I understand why Mr. Ballantine is keeping you on the proper side of the fence."

Mr. Wente stepped into the small yard and gazed about. "Nice place you have here, Ballantine," he commented. "I prefer a comfortable chair and a fire and a beer, however. Shall we discuss our business inside?"

Chet, awed, could only nod. As he led the great executive to the door, he tried to remember the condition of the living room. He couldn't remember what he'd left it looking like. Flustered, he showed Mr. Wente into the living room and saw to his pleasure that all was in order.

"Charming," Mr. Wente said, "I like a man who keeps his place shipshape."

"Well, Abby sees to that these days, sir."

"Abby? You have a housekeeper?"

"Abigail Henrietta Young, your former technical librarian, sir. Abby has the theory that an engineer executive can hardly do good work if he hasn't a comfortable home to come home to. Or maybe she's trying to propagandize me into marriage. I don't know."

"Oh, yes. Well, Ballantine, she's a different kettle of fish, if you don't mind the term. The important thing just now is this lawsuit."

"Abby insists I go ahead, sir."

"Why?"

"Simple, sir. It was all her idea. Diversionary tactics, or something like that."

"I begin to think, Ballantine, that she's outlived her usefulness to the corporation."

"Oh, she was fired, sir. Indigo Norden beat you to that idea, I'm afraid."

"I see. Nothing to lose, everything to gain. Very well. If you sue for three million, we'll carry it to every court in the country – a process that will use up many years and probably break you financially."

"Yes, sir."

"I don't understand this, Ballantine. I've looked into your record. Good record. Now this. Mind telling me what happened?"

"I think Mikel and Norden should be present, sir. Oh, and Deanna, the cheesecake that baited the trap."

"Ballantine, are you drunk?"

Chet sighed. "Sir," he finally said, "you'd be flustered, too, if one of the great names in mechanical engineering popped in on you as suddenly as you've popped in on me. I studied some of your textbooks in college. I came to Better Ways because you were its president. I'm not drunk; just bowled over."

"Rubbish. The textbooks of yesterday are the dead ducks of today, and the fairly competent engineer of yesterday is obsolescent today. I'm glad you told me all that, however. Obviously, your place is still with the corporation. Good. You mentioned diversionary tactics. What did you mean by that?"

Chet said, feeling sophomoric, "My real price for coming back, sir, is Norden's throat. So help me God, Norden framed me! He sent that girl here deliberately to make trouble for me with Mr. Mikel. And she made it, all right, all right. And then Norden, with his lies – well, that's my price."

"Done."

"As I've said, sir, I –"

Chet's mouth dropped agape. He stared a long time. Then, Wente or no Wente, he got on the telephone and begged Abby to come over in jig time.

How it happened that Mr. Wente and he were eating buttermilk pancakes when Abby arrived, Chet never quite knew. Somehow they'd gotten to discussing the technical problem Chet had been working on at Better Ways the day he'd been fired. The kinetics involved had baffled Chet at the time, and he'd been telling Wente why. Wente had at once gotten out paper and pencil and called for a slide rule. After that . . .

Mr. Wente half rose when Chet introduced Abby in the kitchen. "Ah," he said, "I remember you now, Miss Young, of course. Well, this has all been quite interesting. I find, Miss Young, that you're a general who uses diversionary tactics. Interesting. I wonder how you ever heard of them."

"From Colonel Delaney, who lives in the boarding house I patronize. Washburn House."

"Oh, do sit down, Miss Young."

Abby sat down, and Chet served her three buttermilk pancakes.

"Mr. Ballantine has asked for Norden," Mr. Wente said. "I've agreed to the terms. Apparently he didn't feel authorized to sign the peace treaty."

"No, sir."

"Indeed?"

"Mr. Wente, I –"

Abby broke off, her attention distracted by a sound from Chet. Chet went to the nearest window and gave his head a little thump, as if to clear it. "Norden's just driven up," he

158

announced. "I seem to be popular today."

"I ordered him to come," Mr. Wente said. "I like to dispose of things quickly if I can. You see, the important thing to me is the welfare of the corporation. I think I'm a humanist most of the time, but there are times when the corporation is more important than any person who works for it. Business has to be business on occasion. After all, I do have a responsibility to our stockholders and employees. I hope, Mr. Ballantine, that we can have a business discussion with Mr. Norden. He came at my request."

"Sure, Mr. Wente. I won't serve him buttermilk pancakes, though."

The doorbell rang. Abby went to answer it, and it was interesting to her to see the expression that came over Indigo's face when he saw her. "You get around," he said with grudging respect. "You get to important ears, don't you?"

"Not always, Indigo, but sometimes. Why don't you sit here in the living room? We'll be finished with breakfast shortly."

But Indigo seemed to know only one way to do things: directly, with bravado. He went into the kitchen and smiled warmly at Mr. Wente. "Sir," he said, "I'm glad you've taken a hand in this. In my opinion, the situation was becoming sticky."

"Norden, sit down."

Indigo sat, looking calm and utterly relaxed.

"Norden," Mr. Wente said, "I've had a useful chat with Ballantine here. His version of what happened here one Sunday differs quite markedly from the version Mikel gave me. I don't suppose you'd care to give me your version?"

"It would have to be the same story I told Mr. Mikel, sir. I came here that Sunday for a chat with Ballantine. He'd made personal remarks about me that I disliked. I wanted to know why he felt I was riding to success on the shoulders of the engineers and scientists. I was astonished, because I knew that a year or so ago Mr. Mikel had expressly ordered Ballantine to stop taking advantage of his daughter's inexperience and lack of discrimination. Those are Mr. Mikel's words, sir, not mine."

Like any good storyteller, Indigo stopped to take a few breaths after he'd caught their attention. He smiled faintly, then resumed. "I told Ballantine that for a bright fellow, he could be rather stupid. Ballantine turned on Deanna and asked if she'd told the whole world where she was, or words to that effect. Then Deanna exploded, claiming he'd spent the whole time insulting her because she'd refused to intercede for Miss Young. Deanna told me he'd called her father a bloodsucker and that he'd called me just a toad with ambition but no brains."

Again, Indigo paused. Then, suddenly, he looked directly at Chet Ballantine's startled face. "What else happened between us, Ballantine? All I know is that I told Deanna we should leave and that I told Ballantine he'd had it. Mikel was furious, and Deanna was furious. But, Ballantine, what did I specifically do to you to justify your threat to punch me? All I did that day was come for a talk with you, interrupt a scene with Deanna and take her out of there."

Deep, deep down, Abby felt a stirring of admiration for Mr. Indigo Norden. They'd all been wrong about him, she decided, all the girls who'd ever thought they were personally responsible for his success. Indigo had brains and imagination and courage, all right, and above and beyond all that, he had resourcefulness. And that was why he was vice president of promotions at the age of thirty. You might maneuver him into a corner, but you could never pin him down.

"Well?" Indigo challenged. "I'm here and Mr. Wente is here, Chet. Make you charges and present your proofs."

"It wasn't anything you specifically did

here," Chet growled. "It was obvious, though, that you planned the whole thing."

"How was it obvious, Chet?"

"Well –"

"Sir," Abby said quickly to Mr. Wente, "I have the full, signed story from Deanna Mikel. I'm sorry to report, Indigo, that one of your darlings has finally blown the whistle on you."

He came roaring from the chair. "The lousy traitor!" he roared. "The lousy scared traitor! I told her not to panic. I told her I could handle this. Of all the –"

He stopped, seeing Abby shake her lovely blonde head.

The telephone rang. Abby, being nearest it, picked it up and said, "Chet Ballantine's residence." She listened and then sighed. "Deanna wants to know," she told Mr. Wente, "if you'll spank just her, not her father, for the great wrong she's done Chet?"

Mr. Wente took the telephone.

"You were bluffing," Indigo said flatly to Abby. "You don't have a signed story."

Abby shrugged. "You'll never know now, Indigo, will you?"

Chapter Seventeen

On March first, at quarter of nine, Abby officially turned over control of the technical library to Alice Hull. Alice promptly burst into tears. "It's like a dream come true," Alice said. "I know I'll do a terrible job. I just know it."

"If you have any problems, just call me, you idiot. Rely on Linda Aley for public relations, and you'll do just fine. Oh, and you'll be kind to Sally Washburn, won't you? The poor creature's going through the don't-care-a-hoot phase. I live at her folks' boarding house, you know. Until I'm married and in my own home, I'm at the mercy of the Washburns."

Linda came in, wearing a neat brown suit that befitted a person of her august station. "An office boy's waiting to help with your gear," Linda said. "I would've been glad to help, but an assistant librarian can't be seen doing manual labor and such."

Abby patted the girl's cheek affectionately. "Dream on," she crooned. "Some day the girl will be a woman, and then she'll discover a very beautiful reality. Care to know what the reality is? It doesn't matter what you do as long as you do it with reasonable grace and honor."

"My," Linda teased, "and will I be corny, too, when I'm a woman?"

Abby got out of there in a hurry, not sure she could hold her own with this bright young creature who'd probably head the library one day. She took the office boy into her office and showed him the packed cartons she wanted taken upstairs to Mr. Cleary's offices in the executive suite. She herself went to the drugstore on the corner for a bracing cup of coffee and a chance to collect her nerves and her wits for the great adventure just ahead. It seemed very strange to her that all the years devoted to the study of librarianship should have brought her to this moment of saying hail and farewell to catalogues and abstracts and stacks and reviews and reference sources. She was still not certain that Mr. Cleary's idea had been a good one. What on earth did an administrative aide really do? How on earth could she be sure that she'd be competent? It was all such a gamble. Long ago she'd decided never to gamble, knowing full well that it had been her father's penchant for taking risks, for abandoning job after job, opportunity after opportunity, dream after dream, that had kept the family impoverished. Colonel Delaney had indeed been right the day he'd told her she was a loner. Practically all her life she'd been a loner, intent upon acquiring the good things for herself, along with a solid security. Yet in the interests of gratitude and fair play, she'd taken the huge gamble of backing Chet in the conflict with Indigo. And now, in the interests of the children she hoped to have as Chet's wife, here she sat on the brink of another gamble. Suppose she goofed badly?

A sad voice said behind her, "Hello, Miss Young. May I sit down? I never hated you, you know."

Abby swung around on the counter stool to see a forlorn face and brooding but still beautiful blue eyes. "Hi, Deanna," she said easily. "I'm so glad to see you. I was just thinking about you, in fact."

"About the idiot I was?"

"Well, now, if you were an idiot, you stand in good company, if I may say so myself. Welcome to the legion of young and beautiful women who were enchanted out of their senses by Indigo Norden. I'll buy the coffee. That's traditional, by the way. The girl he abandoned for me bought coffee for me when I was abandoned for you."

"That – that person!"

"Now, now. Is the age of chivalry dead? And why can't women be as chivalrous as most men are? We owe Indigo a debt, you

165

and I and all the others. We met him as inexperienced girls; we were women when it ended. And we must be fair, too. At a certain time in life, the illusion of romance is infinitely better than the real thing; say when one is too young and inexperienced to handle the real thing. Now be honest, as I try to be honest. Did Indigo ever treat your person with other than complete respect? I found I could go anywhere with Indigo without having to battle, as it were, for my honor."

"Well, that way he behaved very well."

"So there you are. The rest doesn't matter. I'll be used and you'll be used more than once between now and the grave. I've already forgiven him that."

"Poor Daddy. It just about broke his heart when I told him everything. Daddy knew Mr. Wente was talking to Chet. That's why I telephoned. Daddy made me."

"I'd like to think you wanted to telephone."

"I have to be honest," Deanna said. "I didn't want to telephone. I knew it would hurt Indigo, and I didn't want to hurt him. Isn't that cockeyed? He'd told me there wasn't a chance now that he'd marry me. Even so, I didn't want to hurt him."

"What do you do now?" Abby asked, wanting to change the subject. "Why don't

166

you go to college and learn to do something useful, something important?"

But the beautiful young redhead wasn't ready for that yet. "Oh," she said with a smile, "I've decided I'll have to take a trip around the world. I know it'll be a dreadful bore, but I can't just sit around Cantwell, Massachusetts, and brood about Indigo."

"Lovely work, if you can get it."

"Miss Young?"

"No."

"How do you know what I'm about to ask?"

"It's in your sad little eyes, Deanna. You'd like to pick Humpty-Dumpty up, fit all the pieces back into place, then turn the clock back to last October or thereabouts. You miss the walks with Indigo, the boating with Indigo, the drives with Indigo. You miss the dancing and the poetry. You miss the deep talk about the meaning of life, one's duty to oneself and society. And most of all, I think, you miss the never-never land of your dreams."

"Well . . ."

The counter attendant came along and asked, "More coffee, Miss Young?" Abby checked the clock and gulped the last cold drops in her cup. "Onward and upward," she said. "Good luck to you, Deanna."

By running, she reached her new desk in

her new office only twenty minutes late.

Mr. Cleary stepped in a half-minute later, followed by two office boys who were trundling a heavy wooden file cabinet they'd mounted on a platform dolly. Mr. Cleary glanced around the office and elected to have the cabinet placed between the door and the corner windows. "I think you'll be busy," he said with a satisfied air. "I may as well inform you, Miss Young, that the responsibilities of my position have been broadened."

"Congratulations, sir."

Mr. Cleary motioned for her to sit down. After the office boys had left, he straddled a chair and said, "It won't be necessary for you to rise, Miss Young, each time I enter your office. As I've told you, I expect a hard day's work for a generous day's pay. Manners cost money because they consume valuable time. Now, then. In confidence, strict confidence, mind you, certain organizational changes will be made here over the next three months. Norden is out, of course. He's getting his walking papers now. And in late April or early May, we'll group several departments under the leadership of Mr. Mikel. This will leave the post of executive vice president open. Mr. Wente has invited me to accept that post. I've agreed to do so."

"I see, sir. Congratulations, sir."

"I'm not entirely happy about the situation, Miss Young. I deeply regretted Mikel's impulsiveness. I had thought him the ideal successor to Mr. Wente. But impulsiveness can be a fatal weakness, Miss Young, in any man who aspires to a corporate presidency. The corporation just has to come first in an executive's thinking. The welfare of many thousands of employees is involved in every executive decision, you know. So ... well, there you are. Now about that file cabinet. It contains detailed information on all aspects of the corporation's work. You're to spend the next several months becoming completely familiar with that material. By July last, I'll want a hundred-page brochure ready for distribution to all stockholders of record. Miss Young, we are expanding! We must seek additional capital for a major expansion. The brochure will initiate the drive for that capital."

Abby nodded, deeply thrilled, deeply honored, deeply frightened.

Mr. Cleary stood up, "You'll not marry until next year, I understand?"

"I'll marry tomorrow if I can wangle it, sir. But Chet's such a conservative. I can promise you this, however: I certainly won't let you down or leave you in the lurch. I – sir, I've always been most grateful for your patience with me, your understanding of my problems."

"Well, you earned it, Miss Young. You've always been a worker. Whether we get ahead or fall behind depends upon our industry and imagination, I think. I'm particularly happy to have your imagination in my office. It's a pleasant change."

He left, and Abby had a half-hour alone with the big file cabinet. Then there was a knock, and in stepped Indigo Norden. His face was flushed; his fine gray eyes looked glazed; his smile looked glassy. "Yay, bo," he said, sitting against the wall. "Yay, bo."

"I'm sorry, Indigo."

Nothing could shake that terrible, glassy smile of bravado. "I sincerely think," Indigo said, "that this corporation is now on the skids. I know that Wente thinks he fired me, but what really happened is that mentally I'd already quit."

"Sure, Indigo, sure."

He began to spin the fedora he never wore around and around on his forefinger. "Yay, bo," he said. "Yup, yay, bo. I couldn't marry for the ball of wax, you understand. I couldn't marry any of them even for a shot at the ball of wax. A man has his self-respect. A man respects girls, too. I've always sincerely respected girls."

Abby came close to crying for him then. "I know, I know," she said fiercely. "Don't you think I know?"

Indigo raised his left hand and pointed a forefinger at her melodramatically and said, "I put my curse on you and yours now and forever, doll baby. You broke Indigo Norden. You forced her pride to demand marriage right now, so you broke Indigo Norden."

"You wouldn't stop, Indigo. You just wouldn't stop. First Chet was fired. Then I was fired. You didn't know when to stop."

"I have spoken. Yay, bo, I have spoken."

Abby stood up. "Want me to write some résumés for you, Indigo? I'm fairly good at that."

"No. You have to find the right company, you see; the right combination of circumstances. A man can't just go into General Motors, say, and ease the competition to one side just like that. You need a certain type of company, a dynamic one in full expansion. Then you need a lot of fuddy-duddies for competition. And then you need –"

"Young and lovely girls standing on tiptoe in their breathless eagerness for romance?"

He smiled. "To me, doll baby, all women are young and beautiful."

Abby wondered if just possibly he sincerely meant that, believed it. Perhaps *there* was the secret of his capacity to charm, to ensnare, to use.

"Well," she said, "good luck to you, Indigo. If ever you need help – or even money – just send me a wire."

He stood up. The door opened behind him and Chet came in, sans jacket, his white sleeves rolled up, a green visor shielding his eyes. Indigo studied him as he might study some odd form of insect life. But Indigo had never been a man to waste time on people not useful to him. He walked to the door. He turned, that terrible glassy smile still on his face. "Yay, bo," he said, then was gone.

Why she began to cry, Abby never knew. She did begin to cry, however, and Chet hurried to her and made her sit down. First he scolded, and then he soothed. "Why cry over that guy?" he scolded. "He's trouble wherever he goes. Good riddance to him. And will you just listen, dearest? Sure I love you. Sure we'll be married whenever you wish. I'll even wash dishes after dinner each evening, how's that?"

"He's finished, Chet."

"Oh, come now."

"Don't you understand? A woman defeated him. A *woman*."

"Hang it, I'll *get* him a job."

Chet looked so alive and handsome, suddenly, in his eagerness to do anything for her, even *that;* and Chet looked so beautiful suddenly, so worth-while suddenly, that the tears ended. "I'd like to say," Abby heard herself say, "that you're a fine man, Chet Ballantine."

Then, anxious to get all unpleasantness behind her, anxious to get to the happiness she'd found, Abby got up and walked quickly and proudly straight into his arms.

The publishers hope that this book has given you enjoyable reading. Large Print Books are specially designed to be as easy to see and hold as possible. If you wish a complete list of our books, please ask at your local library or write directly to: Curley Publishing, Inc., P.O. Box 37, South Yarmouth, Massachusetts, 02664.